An
Unusual
Courtship

M/M Regency Romance

Katherine Marlowe

Honeywine Publishing
www.HoneywinePublishing.com
Boulder, Colorado

ISBN: 1517595770
ISBN-13: 978-1517595777

CONTENTS

1

New Tenants at Linston Grange

The bees were in the lilacs as Percival made his way along the Linston Village road. A particularly fat bumblebee looped sleepily across his path, and then latched on to a spill of flowers that hung down over the stone wall along the road.

Healthy and in excellent spirits, Percival Valentine twirled his cane as he walked, overseeing everything in the parish with an approving eye. The new spring lambs gambolled happily in the meadows, and all the fields were green with fresh growth. Everything, it seemed to him, was in order, with the exception of Mrs. Hartley's roof.

He frowned as he approached Mrs. Hartley's cottage, finding that the damage was more extensive than he had expected. The recent storm had blown down several limbs from the tall oak tree that stood next to her house, one of which had gone fully through the roof and remained there, sticking out in an indignant tangle of leaves and branches.

Rapping politely at her door, Percival sorted mentally through what would need to be done. Mr. Rackham and his son would be best for the work. They might rig up a winch to remove the intruding branch, and Percival trusted to their good sense in the matter of roof repair.

The woman who answered the door was round and smiling, and she invited Percival in at once, clucking at him to sit while she put the kettle on and set about making coffee. "Mr. Valentine, how good of you to come so quickly. I've asked Mr. Green to come around with his ladder and rig up a tarpaulin over the hole before it goes and rains."

"I'm glad for that," Percival said. He took his hat from his dusky ginger hair and stooped slightly as he stepped through her door, which had been built for a shorter man than himself, into a kitchen hung liberally with drying herbs from Mrs. Hartley's garden. He kept his head ducked until he had seated himself safely at the kitchen table. "I shall speak to Mr. Rackham about removing the branch and repairing the hole, I'm certain that he and his son will see to it gladly."

"That's very good of you, Mr. Valentine," Mrs. Hartley said. "What a crash it was, you know! I was all cosy in my bed, little bothered by the rainstorm but for the thought that we might need to build an ark if it kept on in that manner! Just drifting off to sleep, peaceful as anything, when it crashed in with such a ruckus I thought that judgement day had come and oh I hadn't gone to church this week!"

The oaken instigator of such crash lurked leafily in one corner of the kitchen roof, eavesdropping on their conversation like a nosy neighbour.

"I've always been partial to the thought that God might be forgiving of us missing one or two Sundays," Percival said.

"Oh, to be sure, but when one is awoken with an unholy ruckus in the dead of night, you count up your sins right quick, Mr. Valentine!"

Percival laughed and propped his chin on his hands, enjoying Mrs. Hartley's convivial company.

"But I said to myself, I did," Mrs. Hartley set down the cup of coffee within his reach, already doctored to his taste with generous amounts of sugar and milk, "our Mr. Valentine will see to it right away, and here you are, just the next day, even with your new tenants to be seen to."

Percival choked on his first sip of coffee. "The new tenants, Mrs. Hartley?"

"Oh, yes, Mr. Green was telling me about it, their carriage arrived just this morning at the Grange. A young lady and two young gentlemen, all three of them very elegant, that's what Mr. Green said, the very height of the ton, a piece of the *beau monde* right here in our Linston."

Percival cleared his throat, still coughing a bit on the coffee. "Just this morning?"

"Oh, yes." Mrs. Hartley beamed, and then all at once her eyes went wide. "Oh! Oh, you didn't know. Didn't they send anyone to tell you? Oh, but here you are, and how would they find you? Dear me, Mr. Valentine, yes, just this morning."

Swallowing a large gulp of coffee, Percival got to his feet. "Then I must see to them at once." He kissed Mrs. Hartley's round cheek, being thoroughly fond of the older lady, whom he had known all his life. "But not until I have seen Mr. Rackham and secured his promise that he will see to your roof."

"What a dear you are, Mr. Valentine," said Mrs. Hartley, blushing at receiving a kiss from such a handsome young man, which had been her reaction since he began the habit at the age of three. He was, in Mrs. Hartley's opinion, quite a bit taller but no less charming.

Donning his hat, Percival tipped it to her and took his leave.

Linston Grange was on the far side of the village, and just as far on foot as it would be to return to his own residence at Linston Manor, so there was little use in turning back to fetch a horse. Percival thought that the walk might suit him, so long as it did not rain, and there was still the matter of Mr. Rackham.

It had begun to rain, in a halfhearted little drizzle, by the

4

time he reached Linston Grange. He had been reassured that Mr. Rackham and his son would be able to manage the roof repairs that same day, which allowed him to straightaway put the matter out of his mind. Tomorrow, if he were able, he would visit Mrs. Hartley again. There would be more coffee, the roof would be fixed, and all would be well in Linston.

Linston Grange was an Elizabethan estate, considerably more spacious and luxurious than his own Gothic manor, and Percival smiled to see it bustling with activity once again. Servants were at work all about the lovely estate, cleaning windows and airing out linens. He had been by twice in the past week to oversee matters and to ensure that everything was done to his satisfaction. The skeleton staff he had formerly kept at the Grange had been tripled in anticipation of the new tenants, who hadn't been expected to arrive for another week.

Percival hesitated only briefly upon the steps. As certain as he was that the splendid grandeur should meet with the approval of the new tenants, he was not so certain of himself and his country manners. Nothing could be worse, in Percival's mind, than if he should give some unintended slight out of ignorance of modern London courtesy.

The butler, Mr. Elkins, greeted him properly at the door and took Percival's hat and cane. "Mr. Valentine, how pleased we are to see you. I shall inform Mr. and Miss Bolton promptly of your arrival. Ah, Mr. Valentine—" With the utmost decorum, the butler reached out and plucked a sprig of rosemary from Percival's wavy, Titian-coloured hair.

"Oh, thank you, Mr. Elkins," Percival said, smiling at the revelation of this herbal stowaway. "Mrs. Hartley has very low ceilings, you see."

Mr. Elkins, who had been hired and sent up from London only a week ago by the new tenants, looked puzzled at this information about Mrs. Hartley but was too well-mannered to inquire.

Once he had been appropriately defoliated of wayward herbs, Percival was shown in to a well-appointed drawing room and announced.

The occupants of the room were threefold: seated on a couch were a gentleman and lady of familial resemblance, while near the mantelpiece stood a third gentleman of generous height and regal bearing. The duo on the couch were too near in age to be anything but siblings, and their likeness of appearance—both of brown hair and warm brown eyes, with small noses and pointed chins—signalled that they might even be twins. The gentleman by the mantelpiece was dark-haired, with lively blue eyes. His shoulders were quite broad and seemed muscular by the way they pulled at his well-fitted coat, and his body tapered to a fine waist above a well-formed leg.

The butler introduced them as Mr. Bolton, Miss Bolton, and Mr. Everett.

"Good morning," said Percival, and cut a fine bow. "I pray you allow me to earnestly welcome you to Linston Grange."

All three of them stared at Percival in a state of shock for a moment longer than was polite.

"Oh, forgive us!" said Miss Bolton, rising swiftly to her feet. "We were expecting Mr. Valentine. Unless you are indeed Mr. Valentine? Or perhaps you are his son! You must forgive our surprise." She glanced toward Mr. Everett at the mantlepiece. "Did you not tell me that Lord Barham had said that Mr. Valentine was elderly? And here you are, sir, of our own age!"

"You are correct on all counts, madam," Percival assured her, and made a bow. "I am Mr. Valentine of Linston Manor, and also the son of the same. I have inherited the management of the estates from my father, who has been dead these past five years." His curiosity was much piqued by the mention of Lord Barham, Marquess of Linston, in whose absence Percival and his father had performed management of the Linston estates for decades. "Are you indeed acquainted with Lord Barham?"

"We all are," Mr. Everett said. "It is our pleasure to be in residence here at Lord Barham's generosity. Mr. and Miss Bolton are his tenants and I am to be their guest. I understand that he has written to you of the matter?"

"He did indeed," Percival confirmed, with a forthright nod, wanting them all to be assured that he was entirely

7

capable in his management of the estates and that he acted with Lord Barham's full authority. "And it has been my pleasure to coordinate with your staff to ensure that everything is in readiness."

"A most admirable job you have done of it," Mr. Bolton commented. "You should know that Lord Barham himself did express to us that he had always respected the competent management of Mr. Valentine of Linston Manor, which competence, he said, only seemed to increase with the passing years."

Percival flushed with pleasure at the compliment to himself and his father, which was almost the first compliment he had ever received from the strange and distant landlord of Linston. "It has been my honour and pleasure to oversee the Linston estates. And an even greater pleasure to welcome new tenants to Linston Grange. This elegant old place has been too long lonely and empty. She will be glad of such charming occupants."

Miss Bolton laughed with delight at the compliment. "She can hardly have suffered much, when she kept such an admirable overseer. Do sit with us, Mr. Valentine. I shall call for tea."

Guiding him to a chair, Miss Bolton went to ring for tea. Mr. Bolton leaned in at once to chat, while Mr. Everett left his post by the mantelpiece and came over to take a chair by

Percival's elbow.

"May I ask, Mr. Valentine," said Mr. Bolton, "has your family had management of the Linston estates for many generations?"

"Oh, yes," Percival said, sitting up proudly at the opportunity to speak of his favourite topic, which was to say anything whatsoever related to the lands and people of Linston. "My great-grandfather was the last Baron Lindsay, who had the Grange and Estates, but he was the last male heir, with nothing but daughters. I have the Linston Manor from my grandmother, which she held in her own right, but the title of Baron Lindsay is extinct. It was my grandmother and her husband who first had the management of the estates in the manner that I do today, first in the name of the Crown, and later in the name of Lord Barham, created Marquess of Linston."

Mr. Bolton's leaned forward during this recounting with polite and earnest interest on his face. Since Percival's chair faced Mr. Bolton and it was Mr. Bolton who had asked, he spoke primarily to Mr. Bolton, but found himself alertly aware of Mr. Everett, sitting to Percival's right. Mr. Everett leaned his elbow idly upon his knee, chin rested upon his fist. His dark, handsome face was turned toward Percival, steady and intent in a way that sent an eager chill down Percival's spine.

This was not the first time that a handsome and well-formed gentleman had evoked such a reaction from Percival, although he was somewhat preserved from the frequency these reactions by the obscurity of Linston, which had a significant lack of handsome young gentlemen, especially those of noble birth. Percival was quite certain that his cheeks had flushed, and did his best to maintain control over himself in all manageable ways.

Near the end of his recounting, Miss Bolton sat down beside her brother once again, and Percival fixed his attention upon her. The elegant and refined Miss Bolton was of above average height, and her straight white dress, artfully trimmed with gold, served to accentuate her willowy figure. Her brown eyes sparkled engagingly above her pert nose and cupid's-bow lips. Percival was entirely surprised that such a charming young lady of seemingly comfortable means should remain unmarried, when she was certainly old enough to have seen at least a Season or two in London society.

"Do you not find yourself lonely in such a sleepy village as Linston?" Mr. Everett asked. His voice was deep and rich, with what might have been a note of brogue tucked into the crisp respectability of his accent. "For surely there cannot be much society of your own rank and age."

The sound of that voice, so near by his side, sent another chill down Percival's spine and brought renewed colour to his cheeks.

"Certainly not at all," Percival assured him. He turned his gaze to Mr. Everett's blue eyes and found them to be focused upon him with the sort of idle intensity that Percival imagined he might find in a lazy tiger. Clearing his throat and continuing to blush, Percival dropped his eyes so that he might regain the ability to structure his thoughts. "There are an assortment of noble families in the district, many of whom are quite sociable."

Mr. Everett's gaze remained unwavering upon his face. Percival met it briefly and then looked away, fastening upon the much less alarming faces of Mr. and Miss Bolton for a few seconds each before he found his eyes returned to Mr. Everett's face and remaining there.

"And—the—" Percival cleared his throat again. "Indeed, I quite enjoy the provincial society of Linston's inhabitants." He was staring at Mr. Everett. Realising this, Percival looked away swiftly, fixing his eyes upon the carpet out of desperation that he should be too obvious in his reaction to Mr. Everett. "They may not be people of Quality, but I am deeply proud to have the acquaintance—and hopefully the trust—of every one of them."

When he looked up again, he found Mr. and Miss Bolton exchanging a glance, and feared that his lack of experience with the London ton must be quite evident in his countrified ways. Mr. Bolton looked particularly amused: his lips tilted with a smile that was thankfully free of mockery or malice.

"I am certain it is so," Mr. Everett said in his smooth, deep voice. It raised the hairs on the back of Percival's neck, and he began to fear that the colour on his cheeks would be permanent. "As Mr. Bolton did remark, Lord Barham has only ever evinced the highest regard for your—and your father's—management of the Linston estates. Such a capable overseer must indeed be loved by his charges."

Percival looked over in flattered surprise at the compliment and found Mr. Everett's eyes to be as dangerously entrancing as they had been the last time he had looked. "It is good of you to say so," Percival said, leaning sideways in his chair in the hopes that a few more inches of distance between them might diminish the intensity of Mr. Everett's influence upon him. "Truly, Mr. Everett, you—and Lord Barham, I am sure—do me too much credit."

"I doubt that," Mr. Everett assured him. Percival was once again fixated upon Mr. Everett's pale blue eyes, and continued his backward and sideways lean in his chair, trying to maintain as much decorum in his manner as he could remember how to manage. "We have found Linston Grange to be impeccably maintained—certainly your hand is in that."

Percival could not possibly accept such credit. "Of a surety, Mr. Everett, it is Mrs. Eddlesworth, the housekeeper, who must be credited with the flawless condition of the Grange."

"And have you often visited the Grange to ensure the quality of that condition?" Mr. Everett pressed him.

Percival licked his lips, drawn to the elegant line of Mr. Everett's mouth. He belatedly realised that this was an even more dangerous entrancement, and returned his attention to Mr. Everett's eyes. "As is my duty, Mr. Everett, to watch over the estates, but I have always found Mrs. Eddlesworth's management to require no correction."

"I think you do yourself too little credit," Mr. Everett insisted.

"Indeed, Mr. Everett—" Percival began, and then discovered in the most dramatic possible fashion that he had leaned rather *too* far, and fell out of his chair.

This caused a minor uproar in the room.

Miss Bolton rose to her feet with an alarmed cry, while Mr. Bolton knelt at Percival's side to ensure that he was unhurt and Mr. Everett likewise rose to hover over Percival with genuine concern.

"Mr. Valentine!" Miss Bolton exclaimed. "Are you quite well?"

Mr. Bolton seemed to be suffering from a sudden onset of a sort of dry cough, but he nonetheless assisted Mr. Everett in getting Percival to his feet so that they might install him on the much more secure seating of the couch.

"Quite well, I assure you." Blushing copiously, Percival

allowed their assistance. Mr. Everett's hand lingered upon Percival's arm before it drew away, and Percival's arm tingled where it had touched. "I fear that I can sometimes be distractible, and thus clumsy."

The tea was brought in at this time. Miss Bolton took charge of the serving of it and provided Percival with a well-sugared cup of tea. He sipped at it gratefully.

Mr. Everett had drawn over the two chairs that had previously been occupied by himself and Percival so that their little group might chat more intimately around the couch. Miss Bolton took the seat beside Percival on the couch and watched him with stern kindliness.

"I do hope that we shall all be dear friends," Miss Bolton expressed. "The three of us would be glad of your company, and to be sure no one knows the area better than you. I hope you will allow us to impose upon you for a tour of the estates once we have settled."

"It would be my most sincere pleasure," Percival said, already thinking of all the sights he must make certain to show them, and hoping that they would enjoy introductions to the good people of Linston Village. He knew that he must remember that the Boltons and Mr. Everett were his tenants, and required only the pleasure of the estates, while all the responsibility remained his own. There would be no need for them to mingle with the common village folk if they did not so desire. Percival thought this a very regrettable state of respectability, for he was certain that his own life would be poorer without the acquaintance of Mrs. Hartley, Mr. Green, the Rackhams, or any of the other local inhabitants of the village.

"Perhaps tomorrow, then," Miss Bolton decided, "if the weather is good. And if it is not, perhaps you would be willing to help me with a little project of mine."

"Oh, certainly!" Percival exclaimed. He did not know the project, but he was already very pleased with the company of elegant, responsible Miss Bolton, mirthful Mr. Bolton, and the magnetic and intense Mr. Everett.

"I would very much like to throw a party," Miss Bolton explained, "so that we might offer our hospitality and make the acquaintance of all the families in the district."

"How pleasant!" Percival said. "A party at Linston Grange. There hasn't been one since I was a child."

That long-ago party was his earliest memory of Linston Grange, and he supposed he could not have been more than five. He recalled arriving with his parents one night while the Grange had been glittering with light and with the gowns of the ladies. He had been relegated above stairs with the only other child who had been brought to the party, a boy his own age who at once seized possession of Percy's hand and had dragged him along through the upper corridors and balconies so that they could spy upon the glamour of the party below.

The boy had been named William, and Percival remembered nothing more but the way his lips curved when he laughed, and the way they felt against his own as the boy stole a kiss.

"—and so I was hoping for your aid in the planning of the party and the guest list," Miss Bolton was saying as Percival emerged from his reverie.

"It would be my pleasure," Percival assured her, smiling at the prospect. "The Ellises from Larimer are very charming, and we shall certainly want to invite the Earl of Aveton and his sons…"

Miss Bolton fetched paper so that she might take notes as they compiled their list, while Mr. Bolton and Mr. Everett listened politely to the proceedings and asked sociable questions about their new neighbours. By the time Percival left that afternoon, he thought that it was quite the most pleasant day he had spent in quite some time, and was delighted to have his invitation to return the next day.

2

A Game of Chess

The next day dawned dreary and wet.

While Percival was breakfasting, he received a missive from Miss Bolton with the polite recommendation that they might postpone their tour of the estates until a day with better conditions, and her invitation that he should join the three of them for dinner that evening. He wrote back with his delighted acceptance, and then began the composition of a letter to Lord Barham to reassure him of the safe arrival of his new tenants, and Percival's opinion that they were all very charming, respectable personages who would be a credit to the residence of Linston Grange.

The day was very productive for Percival, and he felt quite pleased with himself as he made his way to Linston Grange. He took his horse and went alone, despite the bad weather,

17

since it seemed rather too much bother to prepare the carriage for only the short trip to Linston Grange.

Regretting this decision by the halfway point, Percival arrived at the Grange in a slightly soggy condition. Surrendering overcoat and hat to the butler, Percival's heart lifted to be back in the spacious, well-lit opulence of the grand home. His hosts awaited him in a drawing room: Miss Bolton was at a small table with some papers while the gentlemen were occupied with cards. All of this was set aside upon the appearance of Percival.

"Here is our dear Mr. Valentine!" Mr. Bolton remarked with cheer. "Welcome once again, we are delighted to have you."

"Oh, Mr. Valentine," said Miss Bolton. "Is it terribly cold outside? You must be chilled. May I offer you a glass of claret wine?"

"Yes, thank you." Percival flushed at being back in their charming company, smiling from ear to ear as the three of them rose to greet him.

"I'll see to it, Miss Bolton," Mr. Everett said. He fetched the glass of claret wine while the Bolton siblings saw Percival to a chair. Percival suspected that they might have some fear as to him toppling over again.

Mr. Everett bent to offer the glass. His eyes locked on Percival's, gaze as intense as ever, but also amused and kind.

His well-formed face was very handsomely accented by the long, dark sideburns he wore, and the slightly unruly fashion of his dark hair, which fell over his forehead in tumbling curls.

Percival's heart quickened, and he returned the smile. The claret wine was welcome to help warm him after his ride, and soon enough they were called in to dinner.

The Bolton siblings had brought their chef with them from London, and an excellent table was laid for their meal. There were lampreys in cream and a mutton pie along with an artfully moulded jelly in the shape of a sleeping lamb and a tower of fresh berries. Everything was prepared according to what Percival assumed was the latest fashion in London, on account of he had never seen its like before.

Miss Bolton led the dinner conversation with a recounting of their journey from London and the sights that they had seen along the way.

"It is so very refreshing to be in the country," said she, "London is stifling this time of year."

"And we are so very glad to have you in the country," said Percival. "May I ask, how did you come to be acquainted with Lord Barham?"

There was a pause in the conversation, long enough for Percival to worry that he had asked something untoward.

"Oh, he was our father's friend," said Miss Bolton, with a smile that was charming enough to smooth over the lapse.

Percival smiled back at her, although he still felt confused. "And yourself, Mr. Everett?"

"The same," said Mr. Everett. "It is an inherited acquaintance."

This all seemed somehow very odd to Percival, who thought they were all being so peculiar about the matter that, were they any less charming and respectable, he might suspect them of being adventurers or masqueraders. But the letter from Lord Barham had been in the same hand as ever, and there was nothing out of place in either their manner or entourage. It also seemed peculiar that Lord Barham had rented out the place at all, since he had never taken renters before, nor had he or anyone resided in Linston Grange since Percival was a very young child.

"May I ask about the orchard, Mr. Valentine?" said Mr. Everett. "You seem to have quite a variety of fruit trees, and I regret that I do not know enough about botany to identify them."

"Oh, they are mostly plums," said Percival, "although I believe that one of the former owners of the Grange was very fond of nectarines and did indeed love variety. There are pears, and quinces, apples of course, sloes, and of a certainty at least three other sorts that I've forgotten. You have the orangerie as well, although there is only the one surviving tree, which is grafted lemons, oranges, and bitter oranges altogether. Linston

Grange has fresh fruit in every season."

"It seems that there is nothing that you do not know about Linston Grange," said Mr. Everett, with a warm smile.

Percival flushed with pleasure at the compliment, still quite flattered at any and all attention from the handsome Mr. Everett. "That is too generous of you, especially since I have forgotten at least a third of the orchard."

"I so regret that we were not able to have our tour today," said Miss Bolton. "Are you able to oblige us tomorrow, if the weather is good?"

"It would be my pleasure," said Percival. "Indeed, perhaps the exploration of the region may supply us with several days worth of entertainment."

"I believe," said Mr. Everett, "we would all enjoy that very much."

After dinner, the four of them retired back to the drawing room, where Miss Bolton enlisted Percival's assistance and approval with the plans that she had begun to draw up for the desired party. While the two of them discussed suitable dates and menus, Mr. Bolton and Mr. Everett set about playing chess.

The two gentlemen at the chess game provided some queries and input as to the planning, and Percival watched their game with an interested eye. Mr. Bolton scowled good-naturedly as he played, and seemed to be steadily losing, while

Mr. Everett played with a dry smile on his well-formed lips, and glanced over occasionally at Percival.

Caught staring again, Percival coloured and returned his attention to Miss Bolton and the party preparation.

The game came to its inevitable end, with a victory for Mr. Everett.

"You are too much for me, Mr. Everett," said Mr. Bolton, clutching dramatically at his heart. "The game is yours."

"A rematch, perhaps?" said Mr. Everett. "To regain your honour."

"There's no use to it," said Mr. Bolton, although his smile came as readily as ever. "You should defeat me in that one, and the next. You must have someone else to be your cat's-paw. See if Mr. Valentine will agree to it."

"I shall," Mr. Everett resolved, and turned his pale blue gaze and secretive smile toward Percival. "Mr. Valentine, will you have me?"

"I suppose I must," Percival consented, "if Miss Bolton will give me leave."

"You may have it," she said. "Although I do warn you that Mr. Everett is entirely ruthless at chess. You must play to restore all our honour."

"I fear I have little hope of that," Percival said, as he rose and took his place across from Mr. Everett at the gaming table. "I was never skilled at chess."

"Fie," Mr. Everett teased, "you do but protest out of humility. I'm certain you will have me quite at odds to defend my championship."

This did not at all turn out to be the case. Percival's protestations had been accurate, while Mr. Everett played with a skill such as Percival had never before seen. It seemed to him that Mr. Everett was always at least three steps ahead of him, and whenever Mr. Everett moved a piece, it would two steps later end up providing Percival with some dire inconvenience.

Percival was sure that it did not help that he was so very distracted as he played. More than the chessboard, he noticed how a lock of dark hair strayed across Mr. Everett's forehead, how his fine lips pursed a moment before he made each move, and how, the instant after, he would glance up at Percival with his impossible blue eyes. They were challenging and entrancing, and Percival stared back, lips slightly parted, until he remembered that he was supposed to be playing the game.

It was no surprise to him when he lost. Mr. Everett was very cordial about it, all kind smiles, and Percival almost became lost in that smile before he remembered the presence of the Boltons.

He looked over to find them engaged at their own game, playing cards with animated pleasure. The siblings both appeared to be happy, charming people by nature, and they jested with each other as they played.

"Another?" asked Mr. Everett. His eyes were full of friendly challenge, and Percival smiled.

"Another."

He lost the second game as well, after which Miss Bolton suggested that the four of them play at Whist. They arranged themselves around the table with some discussion: Miss Bolton desired to be partnered with her brother, and Mr. Everett playfully objected to this on the grounds that it gave them unfair advantage. Miss Bolton insisted that any possible advantage conveyed by sibling familiarity was a perfectly just advantage, considering the necessity of reclaiming honour since Mr. Everett seemed resolved to continue trouncing them all at chess.

Mr. Everett played the rube, jestingly going on about how very puzzling the game was to him, and ended up achieving victory for himself and for Percival nonetheless, to a chorus of friendly complaints from the Boltons.

It was very late when Percival made his departure for the evening. Mr. Everett tried to insist that he would see Percival safely home, but Percival would have none of this and departed alone, finding that he smiled all the way home.

Percival retired at once to his room, dressing for bed but then instead donning a dressing gown and moving to his study. Excitement and concern weighed heavily on his thoughts.

His heart beat quickly every time he thought of the way that Mr. Everett had looked at him with that warm, teasing, intent gaze. He had never encountered anyone with such a gaze before, or at least had never had such a gaze trained on him. Mr. Everett's lips were almost as distracting, prone to wry half-smiles and clever, gentle words.

Striving to put Mr. Everett from his mind, he reviewed the papers sent to him by Lord Barham's solicitor. Everything seemed to be in order, and Lord Barham's handwriting was easy for Percival to recognise. The Boltons were to reside in Linston Grange. The rental account had been settled in London between the Boltons' bank and Lord Barham's solicitor, so there would be no need for Percival to collect rents from them.

There was something odd about the whole thing. Their familiarity with Lord Barham was significant, and yet they all three avoided Percival's questions on the topic.

He had a wild notion that, if masqueraders, the Boltons could have forged all the documents and the solicitor would be none the wiser. This seemed impossible to suspect of such polite, decent people as the Boltons, but Percival liked to be certain of things. To satisfy his curiosity without giving any hint of suspicion, Percival composed a letter to Lord Barham's solicitor on a minor issue, regarding how he should handle the produce from the orchard while the new tenants were in residence: should they have full enjoyment of the orchard? Or should Percival continue having the fruit harvested and used or sold as was his previous custom? Or perhaps some reasonable compromise?

Pleased with this bit of subterfuge, especially since it would settle an important question, Percival sealed the letter and set it aside to be sent.

His skin tingled with the memory of Mr. Everett's touch. Cheeks heating at once, Percival shook his head to dismiss the intrusive thought. If his skin should be tingling with the memory of anyone's touch, and if he were to be preoccupied about anyone's eyes and lips, it ought to be the lovely and presumably eligible Miss Bolton.

Percival thought it entirely possible that Mr. Everett might have some claim upon her, but no such thing had been mentioned to him, and Mr. Everett did not behave toward her in the way that Percival would expect of an affectionate suitor. In fact, he seemed hardly to notice Miss Bolton in any manner but that of a brother, and certainly paid her less attention than her actual brother.

Taking out another sheet of paper, Percival titled it to his cousin Agatha in London, who would be glad to make discreet inquiries on the topic of Miss Bolton's availability and suitability to be courted by a gentleman of Percival's standing. He set that aside to be finished in the morning, and betook himself to bed.

Much more satisfied with his ignorance now that he had arranged for these correspondences to lighten it, Percival crept under the covers and thought resolutely of Miss Bolton until he fell asleep.

3
Linston Village

Percival woke to a bright, sunny morning with clear skies. Smiling with high spirits, he finished his correspondence over breakfast and then made his way over to the Grange to reunite with his new friends. The butler showed him in, and Percival encountered Mr. Everett in the foyer.

"Mr. Valentine," Mr. Everett said. He was putting on his gloves as he descended the stairs. Greeting Percival with his usual warm smile, Mr. Everett came to stand by him. He stood very close, and although Percival was nearly the tallest man in the village, Mr. Everett was larger in both height and the breadth of his shoulders. "How glad am to see you. I do hope that you're here for the promised tour?"

"I am," Percival confirmed. He smiled at Mr. Everett in return, heart fluttering at Mr. Everett's near proximity. "I hope you'll forgive me arriving unannounced. I do not believe that we decided on a particular time."

"My dear Mr. Valentine." Mr. Everett paused, securing his second glove with a little tug. The gloves were very well fitted to his large hands, and very white. They were much whiter than Percival's gloves, which had seen several years of wear and were only ever brought out at all for occasions when he expected to encounter people of Quality. Percival put his hands behind himself to hide them. He strove not to let his mind wander onto topics such as the strength of Mr. Everett's hands, the softness of his gloves, and the way that hand and glove might feel while clasped around Percival's hand.

Gloves secured, Mr. Everett returned his full attention to Percival. His smile was as dazzling and charming as ever. "I hope I may speak for the Boltons as well when I say that your presence is always welcome, even unannounced."

"May I ask how you did come to know the Boltons?"

"You may. Our fathers were friends, as I believe we have mentioned—or at least we mentioned our inherited acquaintance with Lord Barham. Horatio and Hermione are like siblings to me."

Percival ascertained that these were the Boltons' Christian names.

Miss Bolton at this point leaned over the upper railing of the stairwell and smiled down upon them. "Mr. Valentine! I had thought I heard your voice."

"Good morning, Miss Bolton!" Percival called.

She descended to join them. "I am glad it is you conversing with Mr. Everett and not my brother. If Horatio had outpaced me in the morning I don't believe I should ever recover from the shock. He will join us shortly, I am certain." Her small, pink lips quirked with amusement. "Or lately. My dear brother is ever such a dandy."

Percival did not comment, since the three of them all seemed devilishly modish to his country eye, and he did not perceive any particular distinction between the dandyism of Mr. Bolton or that of Mr. Everett. He smiled nonetheless, in order to be in on the conspiracy of the jest.

"Will you join us for breakfast, Mr. Valentine?" Miss Bolton asked.

"I have breakfasted already, but I will join you gladly," Percival said.

Miss Bolton took Percival's arm, and the three of them went in to breakfast.

"I hope," said Miss Bolton, over an amply-provisioned table of meats and breads, "since you are here so early, that we shall have our tour today?"

"That is my sincere intent," Percival said. "I thought that we ought to start with the village proper. You may care to make the acquaintance of the locals, who are all very kindly, and we must visit the village church. There's the chapel in the Grange, of course, but the church in the village—have you seen it?—is of the most decadent gothic construction, very ambitious for as small as it is. I would make so bold as to say that it is the grandest small church in Warwickshire, but I do confess that I am biased, for I most firmly believe that Linston is the most charming village in all of England."

"From what I have seen," said Miss Bolton, "it is indeed very charming, and you shall have every opportunity to provide evidence over the course of our tour. I am sure that by the end of the week you shall have us entirely swayed to your way of thinking."

Percival beamed with pleasure, delighted at the prospect of sharing his beloved Linston with new admirers. "Oh, and if any of you are students of history—I don't suppose any of you are students of history?"

Mr. Everett smiled over his cup of tea and nodded. "I do fancy myself so."

"Linston has some old Saxon fortifications which may interest you," Percival said. "And there are even the remains of a Roman fortress out in Mr. Carlton's skirret-field, although there's little left of the fortress but a pile of stones."

"I would very much like to see those," Mr. Everett said. His smile widened with pleasure. Percival returned the smile, basking in Mr. Everett's attention until he remembered that he had been in the midst of planning the subjects of their tour.

"If I may keep you from your cook for the luncheon hour, perhaps we might take our repast at Mrs. Pearce's inn. Mrs. Pearce does a mutton in Jamaica peppers which I am certain will delight all your senses."

"Indeed we must!" Miss Bolton agreed. "I shall have our butler, Mr. Elkins, send ahead to inform her of our intent."

Mr. Bolton came in at that point, yawning sleepily. He grinned to see Percival, and made an attempt to quickly hide his yawns. "Mr. Valentine! How glad we are to have you back. I see that Mr. Everett's scowls haven't frightened you off yet."

Percival looked between Mr. Bolton and Mr. Everett in puzzlement. "*Does* he scowl?"

"Oh, most terribly," Mr. Bolton averred, taking his seat and reaching for the pot of tea. "Do, Mr. Everett, give us one of your scowls."

The look which Mr. Everett bestowed upon Mr. Bolton was not so much a scowl as it was a long-suffering, befuddled smile.

"Ah, there!" Mr. Bolton said, and played at swooning. "Gad, if looks could kill!"

Miss Bolton gave her brother a reprimanding little frown. "I hope you will forgive my brother his whimsy, Mr. Valentine." She sighed over-dramatically. "I fear our parents were not stern enough with him."

33

"That is almost certainly the case," Mr. Bolton said, swallowing back his tea nearly at a gulp and immediately refilling the cup.

"Mr. Valentine shall take us on our tour as soon as you have breakfasted, Horatio," Miss Bolton said. "He was just telling us of Mrs. Pearce, the innkeeper, and her skill at preparing mutton, so we have resolved to descend upon her for lunch."

"I am so grateful," Mr. Bolton said to his sister with his usual sense of whimsy, "that you have the sense to plan for lunch before I have even breakfasted."

An amused smile twitched at Miss Bolton's lips. "My dear Horatio, if I waited to plan things until after you had breakfasted, I should never get anything done."

Percival also smiled, partly from amusement and moreso from pleasure that he had been so accepted into their company that the three of them felt comfortable making familiar jests between themselves in his presence.

"Here now, have you three breakfasted already?" Mr. Bolton said, beginning to butter a piece of toast.

Mr. Everett gave short, breathy laugh that was no less charming for its brevity, and joined wholeheartedly in Miss Bolton's teasing of her brother. "My dear friend, the whole world has breakfasted already."

"That is dreadfully pre-emptive of them," Mr. Bolton said, seizing upon a second piece of toast and piling bacon between the two. "See here, let's be on our way. I would not want my breakfast to stand in the way of our lunch."

"Mr. Valentine," said Miss Bolton, smiling light-heartedly, "are you prepared to overlook my brother's lack of social graces if he brings his breakfast with us?"

Percival pressed his hand over his heart and endeavoured to look grave. "I am prepared."

"Then we may begin our tour," she decided, rising to her feet.

The group returned to the foyer, donning hats and gloves.

"Mr. Valentine, advise us," Miss Bolton prevailed upon him. "Shall we take the carriage?"

"If it please you," he replied. "It is my habit to walk, and it is not so very far."

"Then we shall walk." Miss Bolton nodded her head decisively.

Mr. Bolton wrapped his breakfast in a handkerchief, and munched at it contentedly. As they set out, he offered his free arm to his sister in a cursory fashion. She took it, and made a show of pretending not to notice her brother's poor manners.

In playful mimicry, Mr. Everett offered his arm to Percival. It seemed to Percival that this was rather forward for a three-day acquaintance, especially in the manner that Mr. Everett offered it courteously, as to a lady, rather than the jocular linking of arms which would be characteristic of a lively friendship between gentlemen. He blushed again. Accepting the offer would do little to help his distraction in Mr. Everett's presence, but he did much want to be accepted by the trio, and he was also much tempted by the prospect of being in physical contact with Mr. Everett.

Warring within himself for a moment, Percival decided in favour and seized upon Mr. Everett's arm, although he did endeavour that they should link arms in a manner which could surely only be interpreted as friendly. It helped that they were nearly of a height.

No sooner than this was done did Percival's heart start beating quicker. Mr. Everett's arm was warm through his coat, and very steady. It seemed firm with muscle, which indicated that Mr. Everett must keep himself active in some manner.

As Percival had said, it was not far to Linston Village. Mr. Bolton had finished his breakfast by the time they reached the edge of the Grange's ample lawns and gardens, and almost as soon as they had reached the edge of the village they were ambushed by friendly, talkative villagers eager to make the acquaintance of the new tenants.

Linston Village stood upon none of the Society etiquette regarding introductions, and Percival was pleased to see that his new friends took no offence at the energetic familiarity of the villagers. It took them nearly three hours to make their way from the edge of the village to the inn, owing to how they were invited into five houses and conversed with no less than twenty-three villagers. Miss Bolton bought a bit of lace from Mrs. Green and a sachet of dried lavender from Mrs. Hartley, was promised a jar of honey by Mr. Ottis, and made an appointment for the discussion of the proper composition of rose and apple jelly with Mrs. Fowler.

They arrived at the inn in time for luncheon. Mrs. Pearce received them gladly, clucking over them as she and her daughter served their lunch. Everything was as delicious as Percival had promised, and the three Londoners discoursed with the hostess as cheerfully as if she were a lady of Quality seated alongside them. Mr. Everett wanted to know about the local farms and produce, while Miss Bolton had an interest in Mrs. Pearce's spices and suppliers.

While Miss Bolton was occupying their hostess' attention, Mr. Everett turned to Percival. He spoke in a moderately low tone, so as to not interrupt or draw attention from the other conversation. "If it isn't terribly impolite for me to suggest, it seems to me that many of the houses in the village are very aged. Have you considered asking Lord Barham for capital upon which to renovate and expand the village?"

"Indeed, I have increasingly been considering that," said Percival. "It has been in my mind since I took over management of the accounts. But it would be such a very large project, if we were to really consider the village's needs, so I suppose that I have been putting off submitting the request. Linston Village has not changed in a very long time, and it would require quite a large portion of capital."

"I urge you to do so," Mr. Everett said. His warm and encouraging smile seemed to suggest that he had full confidence in Percival's ability to oversee such a thing. "I would... I would very certainly expect that Lord Barham should agree to it."

"Do you think so? I have been loath to bother him. He is so very often away overseas. I have often felt foolish bothering him with the petty matters of Linston Village when a man of such importance no doubt has far more important business and investments to manage in London and overseas."

"Of a certainty, Linston is Lord Barham's seat, and the source of his title. He would want it to do him credit. Besides, as you have said, Linston is the most charming village in all of England, and so we certainly could not allow it to fall behind in any category."

"Oh, that is true!" Percival's eyes widened, already reevaluating what improvements might be required in the village if he considered the matter from the standpoint of what would do most credit to the eminent Lord Barham. "You have me entirely convinced on the matter. I shall write to him at once."

"As shall I," Mr. Everett said, "to assure him of your

excellent stewardship of his estates and to ensure his consent."

Percival blushed happily, flattered by Mr. Everett's confidence in him.

"Why are we writing to Lord Barham?" Mr. Bolton asked, having heard only the end of their conversation.

"Mr. Valentine and I have been discussing how best to apply funds toward improvement of Linston Village," Mr. Everett explained.

"How very droll," said Mr. Bolton, who had little interest in the business of managing an estate. He smiled nonetheless, and angled his fork toward a piece of mutton remaining on Mr. Everett's plate. "Do you intend to finish that?"

"I do," said Mr. Everett, and prepared to defend his plate. "Gad, Horatio, has your appetite no bounds?"

"Oh, some bounds," said Mr. Bolton, "mostly to do with liverwurst."

When the meal was finished and they set out again, Percival took the opportunity to offer his arm to Miss Bolton. He was determined that he should take the opportunity to court her.

Neither Mr. Everett nor Mr. Bolton seemed to take any offence in this, and linked arms charmingly as the four of them strolled towards the church. It was, as Percival had told them, a very grand small church, of opulent Gothic construction. The church spire stretched loftily toward the heavens, and the church was decked all about with arched windows in the

Gothic style, each filled with coloured glass panes.

Mr. Everett was drawn at once to the history of the ancient graveyard, while Mr. Bolton wanted to know whether there were bats in the belfry, and Miss Bolton was fascinated by the design of the windows. Percival escorted her inside for a more thorough inspection, and the other two followed in due time.

The interior of the church was warmly lit with the coloured light from the windows, which combined into a sort of honey glow throughout the nave. Percival supposed the lighting had been intentional, and there were plenty of panes with white or golden glass in order to perpetuate the colouring. His guests explored with interest through the lovely old church, exclaiming praises for the architecture. Percival answered their questions about it as best he could, and was about to go and fetch the rector for a more thorough history of the church when the man appeared of his own impetus.

"Mr. Humphrey!" Percival exclaimed happily at the sight of him. "Here you are. May I introduce you to the new tenants of Linston Grange? Mr. Bolton, Miss Bolton, and Mr. Everett. This is Mr. Humphrey, our rector. Mr. Humphrey, I was just finding myself at a loss to answer regarding the provenance of the glass in the windows."

Mr. Humphrey knew at once, and was perfectly delighted to regale the Boltons with the history of it. They had far more interest than did Mr. Everett, who set off to explore the balcony above the congregation. Percival followed after him, since the Boltons were engaged and he supposed that it was his duty as a host not to let Mr. Everett go off alone.

"It is a lovely old church," said Mr. Everett. "You may find me an awful heretic, but I am sure that I like it better while it is empty and echoing like this than I should when it is filled with a congregation. I suppose it is on account of my love of ruined and abandoned things."

"Ah," said Percival, "then how fortunate it is that we have several of them. The Saxon and the Roman fortifications, and a bit further afield is a gorgeous old monastery, all crumbled now. We will have to ride out to it one day. I am certain that you will like it."

"How thoughtful of you," said Mr. Everett. "I am certain that I will."

"Mr. Valentine! Mr. Everett!" Miss Bolton called from below.

Percival leaned over the railing to reply. "Lo, here we are!"

"Mr. Humphrey has offered to show us the village school, which he oversees." Miss Bolton smiled up at them, eyes bright with cheer. "Mr. Everett, I would not want to keep you from your ruined fortifications, which Mr. Valentine has promised, and I know that you have less interest in schoolrooms, as I likewise care little for ruins. Mr. Valentine, will you be so good as to show Mr. Everett the promised ruins? Perhaps we may meet again here in an hour. Will that suit?"

"I am well-suited," said Mr. Everett. "Will you, Mr. Valentine?"

Percival thought that he was rather less well-suited, since this would in no way further his hope of courting Miss Bolton, but he did very much enjoy the company of Mr. Everett, and had no reasonable grounds for objection. "Yes, certainly. It would be my pleasure, and I leave you in very good hands with Mr. Humphrey."

The Boltons went out with their new tour guide, leaving Percival with Mr. Everett. He had a fleeting thought that it may have been intentional to strand him in the charming company of Mr. Everett, but Percival could not imagine what purpose Miss Bolton might have for wishing to further Percival's distraction.

Mr. Everett smiled at him, with blue eyes that were full of pleasure. "Shall we?"

"To be sure." Percival took his arm once again and they went out of the church.

Linston Village only had one main road, which ran through the length of the little village and on past Linston Manor at the one end and Linston Grange at the other. Small paths and lanes branched off from it to the farms and houses surrounding Linston, but none of these lanes went more than a mile from town.

Percival led Mr. Everett along one of the quiet lanes, enjoying the warm, sunny day and the good company of his companion. Whenever he glanced over, Mr. Everett's eyes were very likely to be upon him, so that it did seem that Mr. Everett was paying more attention to Percival's profile than to the very lovely meadows and fields all around them. In Percival's opinion, he could not possibly be more interesting than the rolling hills and scenery of rural England, and he did his best to draw Mr. Everett's attention to various sights as they passed them. There were not many specific landmarks that could be pointed out in the overall loveliness of the Cotswolds, but Percival did his best by denoting the farms by their tenant's names and indicating the branches of the river Avon which were visible from the crest of a hill.

"Was Linston of particular strategic importance?" Mr. Everett asked, while they were still paused on the lane atop the hill.

This seemed a peculiar non sequitur. Percival peered at him in confusion. "What? *Linston*, strategic?"

"There are Saxon fortifications," Mr. Everett reminded him. "And Roman ones, as well."

"Oh!" This significance had never occurred to Percival. "I suppose there are. I confess I don't know. It is rich country, and lovely. And there is the river Avon. I don't... forgive me,

Mr. Everett, I'm no tactician."

"That's quite all right," Mr. Everett assured him. "It is merely my perpetual curiosity about everything."

Percival smiled at him, thinking that Mr. Everett was ever so clever in addition to being very handsome and kind. He stared fondly until he realised that he was staring, then quickly cleared his throat and looked away. Resuming their journey along the lane, he soon drew Mr. Everett's attention to the Saxon ramparts.

The fortifications they sought were just at the edge of the village proper, and easily visible. Crumbling ramparts of honey-coloured limestone formed a boundary between two green fields and dwindled to nothingness at the edge of the lane. A few honey-coloured remnants continued on the other side of the lane, in much reduced profusion.

Intrepid by nature, Mr. Everett mounted at once upon the ramparts, bounding up a ruined set of stairs to the crenelated top and gazed from there out across the countryside. Percival followed at a more decorous pace, being mindful of his clothing.

Turning back with a wide, jubilant smile, Mr. Everett offered Percival a hand up the last section of damaged steps. Percival accepted the aid, and found himself pulled up at once to Mr. Everett's side.

"Here, Mr. Valentine," said Mr. Everett, with an

adventuresome smile. "We are Norman conquerors upon these Saxon ramparts. Shall I be William?"

Percival found himself at a loss in the face of this childlike playfulness in his acquaintance. "What?"

"The Conqueror," Mr. Everett specified, still grinning.

"Oh!" Percival blinked at this revelation, and then remained befuddled. "And what shall I?"

"Harold, perhaps, to defend your native England." Entirely whimsical, Mr. Everett sat back against the edge of the ramparts. "Or William FitzOsbern, if you will be Norman alongside me."

"Come, Mr. Everett," Percival scolded him, unable to help a smile in the face of Mr. Everett's contagious cheer. "Are you here to conquer?"

"No, certainly not," Mr. Everett said, rising to his feet and taking a step forward, backing Percival against the wall of the ramparts. His eyes were intense and piercing, making Percival think once again of him as a sort of predatory cat. "I will only take what is freely offered."

Percival coloured deeply, eyes widening at what seemed the possibility of Mr. Everett indicating some sort of amorous intent.

A kiss, perhaps, Percival thought.

"Mr. Everett!" he said. "You forget yourself."

Mr. Everett stepped back quickly. "Perhaps I do," he said,

and dropped his eyes away. "Forgive me."

A weighty moment of silence hung between them. Uncertainty stopped Percival's mouth, and he stared at Mr. Everett, heart pounding with the yearning that Mr. Everett *would* kiss him.

"I think," said Mr. Everett, with his polite, friendly smile returned to his face, "that I may come here sometimes with a book, to study. Do you suppose anyone would mind that?"

"No, certainly," Percival assured him. "Perhaps the old stones might enjoy the company."

"I hope they might," Mr. Everett agreed. "I know I should enjoy study in such a restful locale. Will you show me the Roman ruins now?"

"I will," Percival said.

Everything seemed almost returned to normal, as they made their way back down the ramparts and further along the lane. The ruins, in Mr. Carlton's skirret-field, were only around the next curve in the lane, set just along the edge of where the bank dropped down toward the river Avon.

What remained of the Roman stone walls were now merely low piles of rubble. Percival seated himself upon one of them, gazing out across the river and the rolling hills of Warwickshire. Mr. Everett sat beside him companionably.

"Would it be rude of me," Mr. Everett asked, "to comment that I do not believe this to be a Roman fortress?"

"What?" Percival looked over at him in surprise. "But it is, most certainly. Linston records do indeed speak of the ruins here as pre-dating the time of the Saxon invasion, of a surety, there was known to be Roman activity in this area, and—"

"Rather I believe it to be a Roman *villa*," Mr. Everett corrected.

Percival stopped himself in surprise. "Oh. Why so?"

"The plan of the building, or what we can see of it. Even supposing that part of it may have been lost from the way the bank there encroaches and crumbles away, it is not laid out with defensive fortifications. It is laid out like a private residence. There, the atrium. These, cubiculi. The peristylium toward the edge of the field."

Percival looked where he indicated, but saw only crumbling stones and pillars. "I confess I don't know the first thing about Roman villas."

"Shall I teach you?" Mr. Everett asked.

"Yes," Percival decided, with a pleased smile. "Do."

Mr. Everett rose and offered his hand, but seemed to almost immediately think the better of this and retracted it, putting his hands behind himself like a scolded child.

"The cubiculi were the bedrooms. It looks as though there are six of them on this side of the house, though the rooms might also have been libraries or drawing-rooms, I suppose. You can see their outlines, there and there. Here in the centre, the impluvium, would be a rainwater pool."

"Why would anyone want a rainwater pool at the centre of their house?" Percival asked.

Mr. Everett pressed his lips together with mirth at the question. "Well, I suppose it's a folly here in England, but, well—I suppose you've had the opportunity to visit Italy?"

It was instantly clear that Mr. Everett was assuming that Percival, like most gentleman of good birth, had completed his Grand Tour of the continent.

"I'm afraid I have not," he confessed.

Immediately realising his mistake and the unintentional insult he had given, Mr. Everett blanched. "Forgive me. Italian summers get very hot, and the shady courtyard with the pool aids in cooling the house."

"I understand." Percival bit at his lip, feeling provincial next to such a fine London gentleman, and stared glumly down into the grass.

"Shall we return to the others?" Mr. Everett proposed. His voice was gentler than it had been.

"Yes." Percival got to his feet, glad of the opportunity to return to the social buffer of the Boltons. When he was alone with Mr. Everett, everything felt more intense, and somehow they both managed to keep making fools of themselves.

They went quickly, and spoke along the way only of bland topics regarding the management and health of the farms in the district.

The Boltons and Mr. Humphrey were engaged in conversation on the front steps of the church. Mr. Bolton first caught sight of them approaching and waved. "Ho, there!"

Miss Bolton turned to see them and waved likewise. "Mr. Valentine, Mr. Everett. Did you have a pleasant excursion?"

"We did indeed," Mr. Everett answered, his good humour returned as he greeted his friends.

Percival felt forgotten the moment that Mr. Everett's full attention turned away from him. As much as he had wished to return to the company of the Boltons and escape the embarrassment of the revelation that Percival was a *very* country gentleman who had not even the benefit of a Grand Tour, he worried that he may have lost Mr. Everett's interest and friendship. Surely Percival was nothing more than any other aspect of Linston: charmingly provincial, but not the sort of person that a gentleman of London society ought ever to take as a friend.

Or to kiss, for that matter.

"Mr. Valentine," Miss Bolton said. "Mr. Humphrey has been telling me that you intend to engage a teacher for your school."

She had her hand hooked around Mr. Humphrey's arm as if they were already very dear friends, and Percival felt a prickle of indignation at himself regarding what a poor job he was doing of courting the lady's affections.

"Yes, indeed," Percival agreed, pushing his indignation aside so that he could focus on his delight in Miss Bolton's interest in yet another topic about Linston. "As soon as the renovations for the schoolhouse are complete. It had been out of commission for years, and ..." It occurred to him that Mr. Humphrey had just concluded giving the Boltons a tour on this topic. Percival reddened and cleared his throat. "And it seems to me that the children of Linston ought to have a proper school."

"That is very good of you," Miss Bolton said.

"Shall we continue our tour?" Mr. Everett proposed. "I would very much like to see Linston Manor, if Mr. Valentine is willing."

"Oh, certainly!" Percival said, glad to have the group back together and to resume his discourse on his favourite topic. "It would be my pleasure."

"Oh!" said Miss Bolton, and frowned. She looked between Mr. Everett and Percival, then shook her head. "No, I fear you must go on without me! I fear I am developing the headache."

"My dear Miss Bolton!" Percival exclaimed. "We shall return you home at once."

"Nonsense!" she said. "I'll hear none of it. Horatio may escort me home. Mr. Everett did so want to see the manor.

I am certain you will have us as guests on some other day, and I am less in need of history lessons and estate quotas than Mr. Everett." She smiled fondly at her friend, and released Mr. Humphrey's arm in order to take her brother's. "Do go on without me, Mr. Everett."

"Do you have any objection, Mr. Valentine?" Mr. Everett asked. "I have already imposed significantly on your good nature today."

This would result in Percival being alone again with Mr. Everett, a circumstance which he had only just escaped. He wondered that Mr. Everett did not take the easy excuse of going with Miss Bolton and ending the tour for the day, which would allow him to escape from Percival's clumsy provincial manners.

Hoping that his blush was not entirely evident, Percival cleared his throat again and nodded. "It would be my pleasure."

"How good you are, Mr. Valentine," Miss Bolton repeated, beaming approvingly upon him. "I wish the two of you the most pleasant afternoon."

"And may I express my hopes for your good health!" Percival replied.

"Simply a matter of too much sun," Miss Bolton insisted. Mr. Humphrey offered to go with the siblings back to the Grange, and Miss Bolton accepted. Percival wondered whether he should have insisted more strongly that he might escort Miss Bolton home again, but the matter was already decided, and the Boltons set off.

Mr. Everett offered his arm. "Mr. Valentine."

Flustered by this circumstance, Percival looked up into his handsome face with the pale blue eyes, and quickly looked away again. He accepted the arm, clearing his throat again nervously.

They made better speed through the village when it was only the two of them. Percival made conversation on general topics about the maintenance of the village and its residents. Several more villagers slowed them to make their acquaintance, but it was less mobbish than it had been with the full trio of visitors. It helped, Percival was sure, that the Boltons were *the tenants*, while Mr. Everett was simply their guest and acquaintance, who might be at Linston for a mere matter of days or weeks, whereas the tenants would be staying for at least the length of the summer's heat, and perhaps indefinitely.

When they paused to speak to Mr. Rackham about Mrs. Hartley's roof, which had been divested of its leafy intruder but still required repairs, Percival disengaged from Mr. Everett's arm and did not reclaim it. Walking arm in arm with Mr. Everett was all well when they were in the group, but on their own it seemed to imply a more intimate acquaintance than just the three-day friendship, particularly when Mr. Everett was merely his tenants' guest.

At last they cleared the edge of the village and were alone on the road toward the Manor. It was not far, and soon they turned off the road onto the Manor lane.

"How did it come about," Mr. Everett asked, "that Linston has both a manor *and* the stately Grange? It seems to me that is extremely unusual."

"I suppose it is," Percival agreed. "The Manor is older, and was once the seat of the Linston estate. It was my thrice-great grandfather, the tenth Baron Lindsay, who expanded the estates and built the Grange in order to have a more elegant, modern residence. This is why it is called the Grange, since it was built upon the old abbey grange—you recall that I mentioned the ruins of a monastery? The monastery had the possession of most of the lands to the east and north of Linston Village, and so the new residence was built upon the old grange lands. They were both the same estate for several generations, but, as I've mentioned, my great-grandfather gave the Manor to his daughter, my grandmother, which she held in her own right, so that when the title of Baron Lindsay went extinct and the estate reverted to the property of the crown, my grandmother kept ownership of the Manor."

"This may perhaps be very forward of me, but if I may ask—does it injure your pride to be obliged to manage the estates in another man's name, when you are yourself of such an ancient and noble bloodline?"

"Oh, not at all!" Percival exclaimed. "I do confess, there are times when I permit myself some phantasy upon what it would be like to be Baron Lindsay of Linston Grange, but, to be sure, I feel no resentment on the topic. It should be noted that I am in no way Lord Barham's vassal. The Manor is *not* a part of the Marquisate of Linston, and—unlike the majority of the lands and village—I am not my Lord Barham's tenant. My management of the estates is not a duty of either birth or position, but rather a *courtesy* rendered in the recognition of a friendship between our houses. The first Marquess of Barham, in my grandmother's time, allowed my grandmother—Alexandra Valentine, née Lindsay—and her husband the management of the estates out of respect for the house of Lindsay. I manage my own family's estate, which is the Manor and some smaller portions of the village and surrounding land, and I receive some percentage of the proceeds from managing the Grange and the lands under the Marquisate, which is an allowance of a non-binding agreement which I or my heirs may dissolve at any time. Or, I suppose, might Lord Barham, but it would be very discourteous of him to do so. And since it does not please Lord Barham to make use of the Grange, or has not for these past twenty years, we are all best suited with this arrangement."

"I understand much better now." Mr. Everett smiled in

his direction, as they passed through the open gates toward the manor.

It was a much smaller estate than the Grange, but very pleasant. Sheep grazed upon the lawn, keeping it trimmed quite close so that it spread out across the meadow like an emerald carpet. The Manor itself stood atop a little hill backed by thick forest. Built of the pale, yellow stone that was local to the region, the Manor crumbled modestly at the edges like a beautiful old dowager trying to hide her age.

Percival loved it all the more for its age and wear. His Manor was eccentrically lovely, although his affection for it was certainly helped along by the fact that he was never personally required to repair the roof.

"How charming it is," said Mr. Everett. "Is it of Gothic construction?"

"Yes, indeed," said Percival. "It was built by the fourth Baron Lindsay. There was a manor house on the site before it, which dated to the eleventh century, but I know nothing more about it and there were no drawings made of the former house. I am quite fond of my Gothic old pile." He hesitated at the bottom of the steps leading up to the Manor. "Do you wish to see the gardens now, or shall we go in and take refreshment?"

"I would very much like to see the gardens, unless you require refreshment." Mr. Everett's smile warmed his eyes, making the blue of them seem warm and summery.

"We shall see the gardens, and then take refreshment," proposed Percival. He led the way around the side of the house to where the Italian-style garden was laid out in an attractive maze of symmetrical pathways around a central, rectangular pool.

As they walked along the side of the lily-filled pool, Mr. Everett inquired about the various botanical elements of the garden.

"I'm afraid I am not at all certain of the varietal of that rose," Percival admitted. "If you please, I can fetch my gardener. Mr. Jeremy is very knowledgeable, and I am inclined to give him free reign in the gardens. I feel that I am not at all a green thumb, and were I ever myself required to make decisions regarding the garden, I fear we should end up with a group of sticks in a pot."

Mr. Everett laughed. "I suspect that you do not give yourself enough credit. The gardens are lovely, as is everything around Linston. You are most remarkably competent."

"Why, Mr. Everett," Percival said, "I do believe you are an unrepentant flatterer."

"Entirely unrepentant," Mr. Everett agreed.

Percival turned toward him, intending to indicate that they should take the right-hand turn down the upcoming path, at the same time that Mr. Everett turned leftward, perhaps to make another inquiry, and the two of them collided.

Breath hitching in surprise, a flush of warmth went through Percival's body. Mr. Everett reached out and clasped Percival's shoulder, perhaps to steady him, and then quickly let go.

"Forgive me, I..." Mr. Everett began.

"Perhaps we shall—" Percival cleared his throat once again, and awkwardly indicated the right hand path.

"Yes, to be sure." Mr. Everett indicated that he should lead the way, and after a brief shuffle as they both strove to politely not touch or collide, they resumed their stroll through the garden.

Percival felt pressed by the need to say something, anything, which might properly address the situation and set them on the right course. He felt that he ought to some way address their conversation by the ruins, or his probably-evident distraction in Mr. Everett's presence, or inquire as to Mr. Everett's opinions on the matter of two gentlemen kissing: particularly as regards to the two of them.

The gardens were lovely in the late afternoon as the trees cast long shadows across the gravel paths. Percival heard a bird singing, distant and alone, from the direction of the forest.

"The Boltons are very charming," said Percival. "I am very pleased to have made their acquaintance. And yours," he added quickly, lest Mr. Everett should think that he was not included. "Mr. Bolton is still very amusing, and Miss Bolton is... is, well, she's quite lovely, isn't she?"

"She is," Mr. Everett affirmed. He seemed as nearly as unsure of himself as Percival, and made a gesture in Percival's direction which was quickly aborted as he changed his mind. "They are."

"Are you," Percival attempted to ask, clearing his throat nervously mid-question, "that is, is she... I mean to say, as you have the acquaintance of such a very charming and elegant young lady, that you might be..."

"Oh!" Mr. Everett said, surprised. "No. No, indeed. Miss Bolton and I are dear friends, but certainly nothing more."

"Oh, oh, I see." Percival felt a rush of relief. He folded his hands in front of himself, fidgeted with his gloves, folded his arms across his chest, and at last returned his hands to his sides.

"Did you intend to...?" Mr. Everett gestured vaguely. His earlier grace and charm seemed to have deserted him and rendered him nearly as awkward as Percival. "Ah, hm, to court the lady?"

"I thought that perhaps I might," Percival admitted. "She is, after all, very lovely, although I do not know her circumstances, and I fear that she may be above the reach of a mere provincial gentleman such as myself."

"To be sure," Mr. Everett said, "you are a gentleman of very good bloodline, and certainly a competent manager of these estates. If the lady pleases you, you should approach her." He spoke more stiffly than was his usual habit, holding his spine very straight and looking away across the gardens.

Percival felt as though he had done something wrong, and supposed that it might be something in the Boltons circumstances or background of which he was ignorant. He felt very foolish, and wanted very much to have Mr. Everett cheerful and at his ease once again.

"Then I suppose that I shall," Percival said. He felt dizzy, and there was an ache in his belly.

"I encourage you to do just that," said Mr. Everett. His voice was very proper and polite, but had none of the intensity or charm that Percival found so distracting.

They completed their loop around the garden, and stood in silent uncertainty by the side of the house.

"Will you come in and take tea, Mr. Everett?" Percival suggested.

"I fear instead that I ought to return to Linston Grange," said Mr. Everett. "I am certain that they will be expecting me for dinner."

The excuse was nearly transparent, but Percival did not question it. "Yes. Of course." He gazed down at the gravel path as his heart pounded against his ribs.

"I hope we shall see more of you soon, Mr. Valentine."

Mr. Everett made him a bow, and departed.

4
The Ball

Over the next week, the group went nowhere unless they were all four together. Every time a suggestion was made that the party should in some way split, it was rebutted. Percival found it entirely impossible to speak to Miss Bolton alone, even briefly. He decided to wait upon the letters he had sent to London with regards to the Boltons, for it would be embarrassing to propose the idea of courtship only to discover that Miss Bolton would be an inappropriate match for him.

The group focused their energies on the preparations for the party on days of poor weather and tours of the Linston area when the weather was good, and the days passed quickly and pleasantly.

Mr. Everett's presence and gazes had become less distracting, and he was less likely to be found within reach of Percival or gazing upon Percival than he had been the first three days of their acquaintance. This felt like something of a loss, but Percival was glad to not be distracted by him and glad that he might focus on the more sensible possibility of courting Miss Bolton. A sort of heavy sorrow hung in his chest, and he worried betimes that he had given some offence to Mr. Everett, but did not let himself dwell upon the question.

The replies from Lord Barham's solicitor and Percival's cousin arrived on the same day. Both of them revealed that the Boltons were considered perfectly respectable: of no particular birth or title, but comfortably well-off. Their parents remained in London and were well-regarded. The senior Mr. Bolton had his income from investments in merchant trade, and Mrs. Bolton was charming and decorous. It was cousin Agatha's opinion that Miss Bolton ought to be glad to be courted by someone of such ancient and noble bloodline, even if Percival was most irredeemably countrified.

A wet drizzle ruled out any possibility of excursion for the group, but once his morning correspondence was resolved, Percival set out to join his friends at the Grange.

They received him in the drawing room, where Miss Bolton immediately engaged Percival in discussion of their party plans. Mr. Bolton appeared restless, sitting by the window and bouncing his leg with excess energy. Mr. Everett, for his part, seemed satisfied to read his book while in the company of his three friends. Only Miss Bolton seemed adequately pleased with the weather, which allowed her to finalise party plans with Percival.

"I think I shall go for a ride," Mr. Bolton announced, and sprang to his feet.

"Horatio," his sister scolded. "It is dismal out. You will catch your death of it."

"Pfaugh, it is merely damp. I shan't be long." Mr. Bolton would hear no discouragement, and took his leave of the group.

Percival saw as Mr. Everett watched him go, and how Mr. Everett's gaze flicked toward where Percival and Miss Bolton were engaged in discussion of room assignments for such guests as could be expected to stay the night. The glance did not last long, and Mr. Everett returned his attention to his book.

Resolving himself that this was his chance, Percival began to consider how he might approach the matter.

"Miss Bolton," he said, colouring and then clearing his throat. "I thought—I thought perhaps I might…"

"Yes, Mr. Valentine?" Hermione prompted, blinking at him with innocent bewilderment.

Mr. Everett snapped his book shut.

Percival twitched in surprise, and looked over as Mr. Everett got to his feet.

"I think I shall order some refreshment from the kitchen," he declared, casting his book down upon the couch where he had sat. "Miss Bolton, will you have tea or coffee?"

"Tea, thank you," Hermione said, looking between the two of them now. She looked as though she wished to say something further, but did not.

Mr. Everett went out.

Percival fidgeted in his seat. Miss Bolton looked likewise uncomfortable, and Percival wondered if she was concerned to be left in his presence without chaperone. Her servants were certainly within hearing distance if she called out or rang for them, and Mr. Everett would return imminently. Percival was aware that very conservative opinions might object to an unmarried young woman in a room alone with a young man to whom she was not related, and the most conservative opinions might express that her brother should certainly not have left her alone in the company of her male friends. Though he was not certain about how conservative Miss Bolton might be—she seemed, rather, to be quite headstrong in most matters—Percival expected that no sensible person would cast any aspersion upon Miss Bolton for receiving guests in her own drawing-room.

"Miss Bolton," Percival attempted to resume his suit.

"Mr. Valentine," Miss Bolton said, her voice rising more than was her usual habit. "Did you tell me that the Ilspeths should be provided a room or may we pack them away home at the end of the evening?"

"Oh, I think they can manage to return home, it would be more important to find rooms for people who have further to travel," Percival replied. "But Miss Bolton—"

"That will be well, then," Miss Bolton said. Her voice sounded strained and her cheeks were coloured.

Percival began to worry that perhaps his suit might not be welcome. "Miss Bolton," he tried again, making it quick so that they should both have the matter over. "I wish to know whether you might be willing to consider my—consider the matter—whether I ought indeed—if you would be amiable to the idea of... of *courtship*."

"Mr. Valentine," Miss Bolton said, folding her hands in her lap. "It is ever so sweet of you, but I must most firmly express that my feelings toward you are entirely brotherly, and I will not consider the matter of marriage."

"Oh!" said Percival. He cleared his throat and likewise folded his hands in his lap. "I—I quite understand. But we are—we are friends?"

"We are the dearest of friends, I assure you," Miss Bolton said, smiling gently upon him.

"I am glad of that," Percival said. "For I do most dearly value your friendship."

"As do I value yours," Miss Bolton assured him. "Now, we

only have three rooms left that are not yet spoken for, but a requirement for five. How do you suppose—"

Mr. Everett returned to the room. He looked them over briefly, and then sat and took up his book without comment.

Percival wondered how they must look, with both of them flying their colours quite clearly on their faces and yet returned to friendly smiles.

"I think," he said to Miss Bolton, "that Mrs. Wittersea's request may be declined, and we may say that the rooms are already spoken for. We will need to apologise most profusely, and she will be displeased, but her need is simply not as great, no matter what her opinion on the matter might be."

He glanced over toward Mr. Everett, but Mr. Everett did not look up from his reading. Even when the tea was brought, Mr. Everett sipped at his on the couch and did not deign to join the others at the table.

Percival worried about what might have put Mr. Everett in such ill humour, and feared that despite Mr. Everett's assurances that he was only friends with Miss Bolton and his encouragement that Percival ought to put his suit forward, Mr. Everett might have some reason to object to the union. The matter was all quite settled now, but Percival had no idea how he might express that to Mr. Everett when it seemed that Mr. Everett was entirely opposed to conversation.

Mr. Bolton returned not long after. He was in much better

humour after his ride, and the room lightened considerably with Mr. Bolton's irreverent mirth. Percival was glad for it, although his gaze lingered upon Mr. Everett, who never once returned the glance.

On the night of the party, Percival was ecstatic.

He had received a letter that morning from Lord Barham's solicitor that he might go ahead with his full requested plans to renovate and expand the village at double the requested budget. With such funding, new houses could be built, existing ones expanded, and the entire village could be improved with respect to the health and comfort of its residents. Percival's mind was abuzz with all the things he might implement, and he spent most of the day planning and prioritising those implementations, until it became necessary to dress for the party.

He had planned to arrive early at the party, on account that he was, in a way, one of the hosts, and he thought he might be able offer some assistance to Miss Bolton in the preparation and oversight of everything that was necessary for the party, but he found that he had been so distracted by his excitement and plans that he arrived only shortly before the party was scheduled to begin.

Everything was in a flurry when he arrived at the Grange. Very few of the guests had arrived yet, excepting those who intended to stay the night. After consulting with the butler in the front hall to confirm that everything was proceeding satisfactorily, Percival encountered Mr. Everett in the parlour.

He looked enchanting in evening wear, as handsome and elegant as a prince in a picture book. Percival had little concept of any of the latest fashions in London, and thus had no idea of how closely Mr. Everett clove to such fashions, but it was his opinion that Mr. Everett was a swell of the first stare, particularly when so elegantly dressed.

"Mr. Everett!" Percival exclaimed, as he made his way to Mr. Everett's side. "How very well you look, and how pleased I am to see you. I must tell you—I must thank you—you see, I have had word from Lord Barham's solicitor—thanks, no doubt, to your good word of encouragement—that not only has Lord Barham approved the renovation and expansion planned for the village, he has doubled the available capital for the venture."

Mr. Everett smiled upon him at the news, with the same warmth and fondness he had shown from the start. Percival very much hoped that the week of cold civility that he had endured was now at an end and they might be friends again. "I am very glad to hear that. How excellent that will be for Linston! And a source of great pleasure for you, as I can see."

"Oh, indeed," Percival confirmed, and began to happily regale Mr. Everett with his plans and ideas. "I am planning to set out at once for London. There are things to be arranged, you see, I shall need to contract a proper architect, and a stonemason—do you think the village ought to be done in stone? There is a local quarry, but perhaps it would be cheaper in a traditional wattle and daub..."

This discussion only lasted until they were distracted by the arrival of more guests in the front hall, which reminded Percival that he had intended to serve as an additional host. They went at once to greet the guests, after which the under-butler showed the guests off to their rooms just as more guests spilled in through the door.

In the next pause between guests, Mr. Everett commented that he wished to go inquire if Miss Bolton needed any assistance with her portion of the preparations and the guests that she was beginning to entertain in the ballroom. His hand touched Percival's shoulder briefly and lightly as he took his leave.

The warmth of his touch lingered in Percival's memory, and he worried that perhaps Mr. Everett had taken his leave due to his new habit of avoiding Percival. It was not a particularly pleasant thought, and Percival strove to put it from his mind.

Mr. Bolton passed through not long after, taking over Percival's duties at greeting guests and sending him to relieve Miss Bolton from what seemed to Mr Bolton as excessive worry over the flower-arranging.

A flurry of last-minute tasks between the Boltons and a portion of hospitality toward their guests kept Percival quite busy for the next hour, and he encountered Mr. Everett only in passing.

The next spell of respite came when the music had just begun, while the early guests were supping at the white soup and claret wine, and Percival found himself upon the ballroom's upper landing in the company of Mr. Everett and Mr. Bolton.

"Mr. Valentine," said Mr. Bolton, as he sipped at his own glass of claret wine and gazed out over the company, "I am sure that I must return to my guests, but I do hope that you will save me a dance at some point in the evening?"

Percival choked on his wine in surprise, and coughed. When he had recovered himself, much reddened from embarrassment, he nodded. "To be sure, if you wish it. I did not realise—why, certainly I had always supposed that it was only a country custom that gentlemen should dance with other gentlemen, and only if there were not enough ladies present for the dances. I always thought that in London parties one should always have precisely the correct proportion of gender for dances."

Mr. Bolton looked charmed and amused by this supposition. "That is not at all the case, although it does indeed depend upon one's Town hostess. Indeed, depending upon the household and the party, sometimes gentlemen may dance with each other purely for pleasure, if they are good friends."

"Oh!" Percival said, and set to wondering whether or not Mr. Everett might in any way be persuaded to share a dance with him. "Well, if that is the fashion in London, then we must certainly represent it here. I would be ever so pleased to have a dance with you, Mr. Bolton."

"You are too kind," Mr. Bolton said, with cheerful pleasure. He made a bow to them both, and excused himself back to his guests.

Percival swirled his wine in the cup and contemplated how he might approach the topic with Mr. Everett before they might be interrupted or separated. He supposed that a straightforward foray would be the wisest course.

"Mr. Everett," Percival said.

Mr. Everett looked over, blue eyes alert and interested, and Percival found himself obliged to pause and clear his throat in his usual nervous habit before he could manage to continue.

"Perhaps," said Percival, "perhaps you might be willing, also, to have a dance with me at some time in the evening?"

He had the pleasure of seeing Mr. Everett redden with surprise in response to this query, which seemed to set Mr. Everett somewhat off-balance. "I will, certainly," Mr. Everett replied, "if... if, I suppose, you are not too much occupied by the attentions of the young women present, and if we find ourselves at our leisure at a convenient time."

This cooled Percival's pleasure, for it did indeed seem that Mr. Everett was doing everything he could to make a polite refusal to the request. "Yes, of course," Percival said. He faltered briefly, cleared his throat, and tried to recover the situation somewhat by commenting: "Surely, however, it would be you who would be much occupied by the attentions of all the women present, for I am common and ordinary in their estimation, having known me all their lives, while you are a handsome and mysterious gentleman up from London."

"To be sure," said Mr. Everett, with surprising coldness, "I would prefer to avoid dancing altogether."

Percival blinked in surprise, uncertain if he ought to take offence. "Why, Mr. Everett, does it not please you to dance?"

"It does, betimes," Mr. Everett said. "But I fear, Mr. Valentine, that I am in an ill mood tonight, and I would be poor company as a dancing-partner."

"I would still have you," Percival said. "If you would be willing. And perhaps indeed it may lighten your mood, for I would most earnestly desire to do anything I might which would make you smile."

That did make Mr. Everett smile, a little. "You are entirely too good and earnest, Mr. Valentine."

"You do me too much honour, Mr. Everett," Percival said. "Certainly I may have some qualities of roguishness."

"I believe it none whatsoever," Mr. Everett said. His smile

was wider now. "I think you are woven entirely of courtesy and account-books."

Sensing that he was being teased, Percival flushed and prickled. "I am—I have other qualities! Indeed, I—I am entirely too familiar with the ladies of my parish."

"Oh!" Mr. Everett said, beginning to laugh, being much returned to his good humour of their first acquaintance. "Are you?"

"I am indeed," Percival insisted, lifting his chin proudly at his very slender claim to being a rake-shame. "I am even so profligate as to kiss certain ladies upon their cheeks."

Mr. Everett gasped and clutched at his heart. "Mr. Valentine! Do not say so!"

"Well," Percival said, since Mr. Everett's play-acting was rather good and Percival entertained the sudden worried notion that Mr. Everett might in fact have believed some scandal upon Percival's character, "to be sure, they are all widowed ladies, and such as I have known since I was the smallest child, for I would certainly never take such familiarity with a maiden lady."

"I am much reassured," Mr. Everett said, coughing as he attempted to quell his laughter. "I think that perhaps I may even deign to continue our acquaintance, despite this most shocking revelation."

"That is very kind of you," Percival said, holding his chin

up, although he was not entirely sure if they had determined whether or not Percival was entirely starched and strait-laced. It worried him briefly that he might have become a matter of sport amongst his new friends because of his pedantic leanings, but he hoped indeed that the Boltons and Mr. Everett were all three too good-natured to make such sport at the expense of their acquaintances.

Percival found himself pulled away from Mr. Everett as the party got fully underway. They were both called upon frequently to dance—Percival on account of being well-known and generally well-liked in the district, and Mr. Everett on account, as Percival had expected, of his handsome face and mysterious demeanour. Mr. Bolton likewise was kept very busy, due to his lively demeanour and wit, and Miss Bolton was in such demand that her friends were only able to secure dances with her because of having prior claims.

The musicians were quite skilled, and Percival was proud of having procured them. Miss Bolton had provided the players with the music of some of the most popular new songs from London, including more than one waltz, but those were interspersed with more familiar dancing tunes. All the country gentry in attendance were familiar with the country jigs that were played, and the dance floor was kept quite full with energetic reels.

Mr. Everett cut quite a fine figure as he danced. Percival

found his eye drawn to him, again and again. There were quite a few dances to be had, and Percival watched his friends and acquaintances with great pleasure. He saw that Miss Bolton danced several times with Mr. Humphrey, the rector, and that Mr. Bolton seemed to have earned favour in the eyes of all three daughters of the Beckinsale family.

True to his word, Mr. Bolton took a turn with Percival. He danced well, with great energy and cheer, and Percival enjoyed himself thoroughly.

The few waltzes that were played were all entirely unfamiliar to Percival. During them, he lingered near the sides of the dance floor, along with a generous contingent of the other guests who either did not know or approve of waltzing.

Mr. Everett found him during one of these. "Do you not waltz, Mr. Valentine?"

"I'm afraid I have never learned," Percival said.

"I did promise you a dance," Mr. Everett reminded him, with a half-smile that hinted at warmth. "If you will take a turn with me, I should gladly teach you."

"I shall," Percival said, although he knew that he might perfectly well make a fool of himself by dancing poorly at the new style. He knew that it had become widely popular in France and Germany, but several of his parishioners were strongly of the opinion that such an intimate dance—between couples, rather than performed in a group, and with the gentleman's arm so brassly enfolding the lady's waist—was a shocking vulgarity upon a polite dance floor.

"I hope you will allow me the lead?" Mr. Everett asked, offering his hand to Percival and placing his hand on Percival's waist. "At least until I have taught you the way of it, and then we may switch off as you please."

"Oh, so you intend to waltz with me more than once?" Percival asked him, smiling as Mr. Everett led him onto the floor.

The question earned a little bit more of a smile, and Mr. Everett's eyes remained upon his face as they swirled among the other dancers. "I think I may," Mr. Everett said. "If only so that you may master the style and seem wonderfully urbane among the ladies of the district."

"You are very thoughtful, Mr. Everett," Percival said. He felt his cheeks warming as they danced. Mr. Everett held him quite close, near enough that Percival could smell the sweet scent of violets and anise on Mr. Everett's breath from the French pastilles that he favoured. Percival expected that he should taste as sweet, and was overcome with a sudden longing to find out.

Mr. Everett guided him gently, giving quiet instruction as Percival followed. He very kindly refrained from commenting about Percival stepping on his toes as Percival clumsily attempted to keep up with the unfamiliar steps.

Their dance ended all too shortly, and Percival felt cold and lonely in the absence of Mr. Everett's arms around him.

Distracting himself by engaging in several more of the dances that followed, Percival kept ever aware of Mr. Everett's place on the dance floor. When the next dance came, Mr. Everett danced with a young lady of quality who was much more skilled at the steps than Percival, and they looked a perfectly lovely couple as they turned about the floor. Percival happened to know that the young lady was an heiress, and thought that they might make an admirable match—although, as it occurred to him at this point, he knew precisely nothing about Mr. Everett's finances or rank, having not thought it pertinent to inquire about the matter when he had written to his cousin Agatha. Percival wondered whether it would be acceptable to put the question discreetly to Mr. Bolton, although truly he had no fair reason for needing to know the finances of Mr. Everett. It was hardly as though Percival was going to marry him, and if any of the young ladies in the district fancied that they might do so, they could certainly do their own research.

Percival danced until the musicians had at last put up their instruments for the night. The dance floor was nearly empty by then, and most of the guests had gone home. Some of the guests had partaken rather too heavily of the rich burgundy wine that was served later in the evening, and the servants were gently escorting such guests to their carriages or up to their rooms.

Everything seemed to have gone quiet all at once as the music stopped. There was no sound left in the ballroom but the whisper of servants and the scuff of furniture being moved as things were tidied away. The elegant, fastidious ballroom had been left in quite a rumple by her guests, but Percival found himself very pleased by the sight of that rumple, glad to see Linston Grange in proper use once again.

Sinking into a chair, Percival watched the guests dwindle away, remaining alert in case his authority was needed, but finding that the Grange staff—more than half of which he had hired personally—knew their business and carried it out with the utmost discretion.

"What shall you, Mr. Valentine?"

Surprised by the question, Percival looked up. Mr. Everett had approached him, and stood leaning against a chair quite near to Percival's side.

"Shall I aught?" Percival replied, not certain what Mr. Everett was asking.

"Surely you cannot intend to sleep in that chair," Mr. Everett said with a wry smile.

"Oh! No. No, I think not."

"Then perhaps you will allow me to walk you home."

"Oh!" Percival said. "No, no, certainly, not unless you will subsequently let me walk you home, and I think that combined journey would be rather too tiring for us both. I shall manage on my own."

Mr. Everett's smile widened with amusement at the thought of the two of them being eternally caught at walking between their two places of residence on account of being so polite as to insist upon walking the other home. "Perhaps, then, I may offer that you might bunk with me? To save you the long journey to Linston Manor so late at night, after a spirited evening."

The suggestion was tempting, but Percival did not at all trust himself to accept, since he did not know how he might react while sleeping next to the highly distracting Mr. Everett. "I could not impose upon you, Mr. Everett."

Mr. Everett looked away, and did not press the issue.

The silence between them felt weighty and painful. Something had been damaged in their friendship, and Percival still did not understand why.

"Mr. Everett," he said softly.

His friend glanced over and waited for him to continue.

"I suppose that Miss Bolton has told you—unless, I suppose, perhaps she did not, in order to be discreet—that I, well, in regards to the matter on which we last spoke, that is, the matter of which we spoke… when we…"

"Mr. Valentine," Mr. Everett interrupted, "really—"

Percival would not be stopped. "But I must—you should know—you see, Mr. Everett, that Miss Bolton declined my offer of courtship."

This was received with a startled silence.

"My sympathies," Mr. Everett said at last.

"Oh. Well." Percival cleared his throat. He had not sought nor wanted condolences, although he realised belatedly how that might be the expected result in this situation. "I suppose I find I am really not so wrenched about it. Although Miss Bolton is really quite lovely, I'm not so certain that I desire marriage, nor that she would be very good match for me, nor certainly I for her, and overall I find myself entirely grateful that we are resolved to be nothing more than the very best of friends."

"I see," Mr. Everett said. Percival could not interpret his expression.

"Indeed, I almost think..." Percival bit his tongue, trying to determine what he was about to say and whether or not it was entirely foolish.

"Yes?"

The marble floor in front of him was polished to an exquisite shine, and Percival suddenly took great interest in it. "I almost think," he said, "that my affections are truly drawn toward a different individual, although I am not at all certain whether such affections are appropriate."

"Not Mr. Bolton, I hope."

The words were playfully said, and so unexpected that Percival brayed once with laughter. "Ha! Oh, no! No, certainly not. Not Mr. Bolton. Though he is likewise really quite charming and were I to be inclined toward either of the Boltons—"

This train of thought suddenly seemed dreadfully incriminating and Percival swiftly diverted it. "That is to say, no. Um. No."

"And if this inappropriate individual were to return your affections?" Mr. Everett asked, taking a seat near Percival.

Mr. Everett seemed earnest about his question. His expression was open and gentle, and he smiled at Percival.

"Oh," said Percival. He cleared his throat again as he attempted to make sense of that in any other manner but the impossible belief that Mr. Everett shared his inclination to be distracted by members of his own gender. "I suppose I don't know."

"Stay the night, Mr. Valentine," Mr. Everett suggested. "You shall share my bed. And," he added, with a teasing glint in his eye, "you have my word that your honour shall survive entirely intact. We may, indeed, sleep with a sword betwixt us if it would comfort you."

Percival blushed and grinned at the teasing, accepting Mr. Everett's hand to pull him to his feet. "I trust your behaviour is above reproach, Mr. Everett."

Once he was standing, Mr. Everett kept hold of his hand, and Percival thought, once again, that Mr. Everett might intend to kiss him.

A servant nearby made a small clatter with a dish and they were reminded of where they were. Mr. Everett released Percival's hand.

"You will stay, then, Mr. Valentine?"

"I will," Percival said. "If you are certain it is no imposition."

Mr. Everett demurred politely that it was no imposition whatsoever, and to be sure he would be glad to know that Percival was safe abed and not at risk of turning his ankle on the country lane on his way home. This set Percival to discoursing on the nature of country lanes, particularly Linston's country lanes, which Mr. Everett attended patiently while he steered Percival upstairs to bed.

5
London

By the time Percival reached London, he was feeling quite thoroughly rattled, and had much remembered why he so despised travelling by carriage.

The streets in London were certainly an improvement than the potholed and muddy country roads, although Percival thought it scarcely possible that anything could be in much worse repair than the rural roads of England.

His thoughts, when he could manage to keep any thought in his head other than frustration at the rattling of the carriage, returned constantly to Mr. Everett. When they had shared Mr. Everett's bed, perfectly chastely, Percival had expected himself to be sleepless due to distraction, but he found instead that he slept at once, and quite pleasantly. Mr. Everett made no improper move, which made Percival doubt as to whether he had ever thought or intended such a thing.

He wished very much to discuss this with Mr. Everett, and thought he might actually make an attempt to broach the subject at some time in the near future.

It would have to wait until he returned from London. He wanted the plans for the expansion of Linston to be put immediately into action, which would require architects and skilled builders, particularly those with experience expanding country villages without any damage to the industry and livelihood of its inhabitants.

Feeling entirely dizzy and ill by the time the carriage arrived in front of his cousin Agatha's residence in London, Percival descended from the carriage and gulped air, which only made him feel a bit more ill. Agatha's town house was in a perfectly respectable part of the Town, but the scent of London and the Thames remained pervasive.

Within the house, Agatha and her husband would be lurking. Percival considered packing back into the carriage and setting out for Linston forthwith.

Steeling his nerves, he climbed the steps and rang the bell.

A butler opened the door and let him in, and showed him into the front parlour to wait. He settled into a chair by the front window, nervously wringing at his gloves as he awaited his cousin.

He had not long to wait, though it was Agatha's husband,

Colonel James Willworth, who appeared first. The Colonel burst noisily through the door and paused upon the threshold to peer at Percival through his spying-glass. Being of ample girth and high self-importance, Colonel Willworth tended to puff out his chest as he strode. Unfortunately for the Colonel, he had rather less chest than belly, which made him appear as though he was going everywhere belly-first. "Percival! Dear lad, here you are."

Making an effort not to prickle at the use of his first name, which Percival had always thought to be very familiar and unpleasantly patronising when it came from his cousin's husband, Percival rose to his feet and pasted a polite smile on his face. "Good day, Colonel Willworth. I—"

"Well, did you send word you were coming, dear lad?" Colonel Willworth cut him off.

Percival bit his tongue and coloured, finding the colonel's tendency to interrupt to be very trying on his nerves. "Indeed, I—"

"The letter must have been lost in the mail," Colonel Willworth hypothesised, being uninterested in any account of events other than his own. "Really, I do think that it is simply intolerable that the mail service should be run in this addle-pated manner! Something should be done. Why, do you know, that last year I sent to my brother, Robert—I think you will remember Robert? He is married these days, to a most profligate shrew."

Percival tightened his jaw and coloured further as he restrained the urge to make a defence of Mrs. Robert Willworth's character. It was Percival's opinion—having only met her the once—that the poor lady was uncommonly patient and long-suffering with the members of the Willworth family, but he knew that expressing as much would make no impact upon Colonel Willworth's perspective, and would most likely bring down further lecturing and wrath upon himself—and possibly, in belated fashion, upon poor Mrs. Robert Willworth herself.

"What was I saying? Oh, yes. The mail. Would you know that he has written to me that my letter from last year has only this month been delivered to him! It's unacceptable! Indeed, I fully intend to—"

Percival was at this point spared from a detailed account of Colonel Willworth's planned campaign against the shockingly irresponsible mailboys of the world by the arrival of his cousin Agatha, now Mrs. James Willworth.

"Percival!" she exclaimed. Like her husband, she was middle-aged and somewhat stout, although she entered any room by the stern thrust of her large, bony shoulders, which made her as forcefully magnetic as she was overwhelming.

"Cousin Agatha," Percival began, already exhausted by the force of their combined presence.

"You wicked boy, how shocking of you to simply turn up like this. Why didn't you write?"

Percival opened his mouth to respond, but was saved from having to do so by Colonel Willworth, who was much loath to let anyone in the room other than himself answer questions, regardless of what the question might be.

"It seems that his letter was lost in the mail, my dove! Why, I'm certain that it's those snitching mail boys again—greedy, lazy sorts every one! It's them that's causing the ruin of this country!"

"Oh! Oh! Shocking!" Mrs. Willworth agreed. "Percival, my poor boy, it's a wonder you survived the journey at all. Did you have any trouble? Why, with the amount of footpads and adventurers on the roads these days! In fact, I quite think that the mail boys are most likely in league with the common footpads, don't you suppose? It would be quite like them. Claim that they were set upon by footpads in order to cover up their own grasping laziness! Lud! Well, I do certainly think…"

This went on for several minutes more between the two of them, while Percival tried not to feel entirely dizzy from his long journey. He wished very much that one of them would eventually remember to invite him to sit and perhaps even to offer tea.

"Here," Agatha said at last, "how long do you intend to stay, Percival? I shall ring for luncheon. You must be quite tired from your journey. Lo! I am quite tired at even the thought of it! Ha!"

There was the briefest pause in the Willworth's discourse as Agatha reached to ring the bell for the servants, and Percival seized upon it. "Several days, I do think," he said, speaking rapidly in order to take advantage of the brief opening in conversation. "Lord Barham has approved funds for the expansion of Linston, and I hope—"

"You always speak so dreadfully fast, Percival," Agatha reprimanded him. "It is a shameful habit, and I do not know why your father never corrected you of it. In fact, I think he was rather shockingly lax with you in quite a variety of ways, but—lo!—it is not my place to comment on such things. Really, I always had my doubts about that man! Ever since he married your mother, my sweet cousin Eloise—oh and she was a headstrong one, wasn't she? Off with him to his dreadful muddy little estate—" Agatha paused here, having at this point crossed even her own extremely lax views as to what portions of her own dialogue might give insult. Her wide face broke into a bright smile, which she probably intended as charming but Percival rather found intimidating. "And how is your little provincial estate, Percival?"

"Quite well," Percival replied, making an effort to speak at a reasonable pace despite his certainty that he wasn't going to make it through three sentences without being interrupted.

"Linston Grange has the pleasure of three new tenants, you will recall that I wrote to you concerning them, and—"

The butler appeared at this point in response to the ringing of the bell, and Agatha immediately transferred her full attention to him and away from Percival, which she would have considered a shameless and unforgivable breach of manners if it had been perpetrated by anyone other than herself.

Percival bit his tongue and waited as she and Colonel Willworth meandered through a decision process as to what they wanted for lunch. This necessitated three entire changes of menu, during which Percival was repeatedly consulted and yet never given any opportunity to speak.

"Here, now, Percival," Agatha said. "Will you sit! I hope you don't intend to keep us standing around all afternoon!"

Percival sat.

"Dear boy," Colonel Willworth said, "when do you suppose you're going to be married? You sent to us with regards to the charming Miss Bolton—"

"Charming," Agatha interrupted, "but of rather poor sense, don't you think? It's well that she comes from money, but that one needs a stern hand, I do think. It's quite a pity you haven't got one, Percival."

"Too true, too true!" Colonel Willworth chorused. "When is the wedding, Percival?"

They both seemed to actually expect an answer to this.

Percival cleared his throat and fidgeted. "In fact, I... Miss Bolton..."

"Spit it out, Percival!" Agatha snapped.

"Miss Bolton refused my suit."

This was received with a shocked silence.

"Well," Agatha said, whipping open her fan and beginning to rapidly air herself with it. "I always said that young woman was of questionable sense. Really, how does she ever expect to get a husband if she thinks—and at her age! She should be grateful to have any offers, much less one from such a respectable family—well, moderately respectable, I suppose..."

"Think nothing of it, Percival!" Colonel Willworth urged him. "You are well to be rid of such an inconstant jade! Really, I do wonder that you should have such poor taste as to have your head turned by a pretty face with a bit of fortune. You need sense, my boy, and quickly! You ought to be married."

"Really, Percival," Agatha agreed, "I can't imagine why you haven't married yet. You ought to have a wife to manage your estates, and you're in such shocking disregard of your duty. You ought to be providing heirs for your lineage, really, what do you suppose would happen to your little country manor if you died without heir? I'll tell you! It would revert to the crown, or, worse, it would be seized by those grasping Barhams! The way they seized upon the lands of the noble Lindsays! Why, when Eloise first told me how it all occurred,

I was shocked!"

Percival thought that his cousin Agatha had a skewed perspective on the events surrounding the transfer of Linston Grange to the Barham lineage, but he knew better than to enlighten her.

"You know, Percival," said Colonel Willworth, "it seems quite fortunate that you have arrived to-day! For we are in fact having a little soiree tomorrow evening, and there will be—won't there, my sweet?—several eligible young ladies in attendance."

"There will!" Agatha confirmed. "Which, I think, is very fortunate for you, Percival. I can't imagine why you've delayed so long in the Season to come to London, as so many of the most eligible young ladies have already been snatched up, but there are still some to be had, and perhaps your trip to London will not be an absolute waste if you do manage to see yourself to a bride. Do say that you will attend."

Percival did not correct her on the point that she could not know whether or not his trip to London should be a waste, considering that they had at no point allowed him to express the purpose of his trip. He gritted his teeth. "It would be my pleasure to attend, cousin Agatha," he expressed.

"Really, Percival! You sound almost resentful. It is my utmost hope that a proper wife will take you in hand and improve your disposition somewhat. Certainly, as I was saying to my dear friend Mrs. Sybil Unston..."

As early as he was able to escape from the Willworths at breakfast the next morning, Percival set out to meet with Lord Barham's solicitor, Mr. Ibrahim.

The man held an impeccably respectable set of offices in Marylebone, and Percival was shown in promptly. Mr. Ibrahim sat behind his desk amidst a small city of neatly-arranged stacks of paperwork.

"Mr. Valentine!" The dark-complected man behind the desk rose at once to greet him with a friendly smile. "Here you are. I have been expecting you."

Relieved to be expected by *someone* in this city, after the well of indignant surprise he'd encountered at his cousin's residence, Percival greeted Mr. Ibrahim politely, and sat down in the indicated chair across from Mr. Ibrahim's desk.

Percival had always judged the solicitor to be an Ottoman Turk, or perhaps an Egyptian, and was extremely curious about what might have led such a man to become a barrister in England—and, further, what difficulties he must have overcome to do so—but thought it would be indiscreet to inquire.

"Now, then," said Mr. Ibrahim. "This is about the renovations to Linston, yes? How pleased you must be! I am sure this must appeal to your good industriousness. I am delighted for you. As you will see, I have drawn up a list of some recommendations of suitable candidates to do the design and construction. Here are their addresses, you may interview them at your leisure. I will, of course, be pleased to arrange the matter on your behalf if you prefer, but I know how you do love these sorts of matters and, of course, no one knows Linston better than you."

Flushing happily at the praise and Mr. Ibrahim's good-natured helpfulness, Percival looked over the list, which had included some notations regarding the known specialties of the architects and masons in question, and some suggestions as to where Percival might start. It was all very neatly and efficiently done, and would considerably shorten the time Percival needed to complete his tasks in London.

"This is very smartly done, Mr. Ibrahim! What a pleasure it is to know that I can always count on you." Percival smiled happily at him, folding the list and tucking it away in his pocket. "You have my sincere thanks."

"It is an utmost delight to see to the needs of yourself and my Lord Barham," replied Mr. Ibrahim. He seemed to eternally be brimming with earnest friendliness, and it made Percival's heart swell with trust and pride in their good solicitor. "Is there anything else you require at present, Mr. Valentine?"

"Well, I suppose," Percival began, and cleared his throat. "I wished to ask… well, I don't suppose that Lord Barham is in town at present?"

"No, I fear not," Mr. Ibrahim informed him, folding his hands and frowning. "He remains upon the continent."

"Yes, of course," Percival said. "I expected as much. Only…"

"Only?" Mr. Ibrahim inquired. His eyebrows lifted.

Percival had never before questioned Lord Barham's perpetual absence from London. He fidgeted. "Only, I did wonder, owing to how Mr. and Miss Bolton do seem to be very good friends with Lord Barham, in addition to Mr. Everett, and I did rather think… that is to say, I wondered whether, I suppose, ah…"

"Yes, Mr. Valentine?"

"Well, I did somewhat wonder how they made the acquaintance of Lord Barham *in absentia*," Percival said, feeling a bit put out that Lord Barham had troubled himself to make the acquaintance of these charming strangers, but had never troubled himself in the past five years to make the acquaintance of the manager of his estates.

"Ah, I see. I'm afraid I am not certain how it was that Lord Barham made the acquaintance of his young friends, nor when. He does not confide in me such matters."

It felt almost like a lie, which seemed so peculiar from the respectable Mr. Ibrahim. Percival frowned, remembering how all three of the guests at Linston Grange had expressed that the acquaintance was inherited, and certainly Mr. Ibrahim would have known that.

"I understand," Percival said. "Perhaps, next time you encounter Lord Barham, you might … indicate to him that I would much desire to make his acquaintance. Whenever is convenient for him. Or perhaps he might care to visit the Linston estates for himself, if only briefly. Surely he would feel welcome there among the companionship of his friends."

Mr. Ibrahim looked down at his papers. It was clear that he was concealing something, and he seemed pained by it. "I will endeavour to do so, Mr. Valentine," he said at last.

There was nothing more to say. Percival got to his feet. "Thank you, Mr. Ibrahim. I always appreciate your diligent assistance."

"The pleasure is all mine, Mr. Valentine," the solicitor said, and showed him to the door.

The party at the Willworth's was a sedately splendid affair, with everything arranged to Agatha and James' exacting and conservative tastes. Percival made certain that his wardrobe was as impeccable as it could be made, since he knew that any flaw in his appearance would be seized upon by either his cousin or her guests as a Mark upon his Character.

After meeting with several architects and masons and selecting a friendly team of them whose qualifications and character were to his satisfaction, Percival had called upon his couturier—or, more accurately, Lord Barham's couturier, who had been recommended to Percival by Mr. Ibrahim in the past. Percival had always been satisfied with the couturier's services—as he had been satisfied with all recommendations ever made by the incomparable Mr. Ibrahim—but he had not had an occasion to properly visit the man in three years, and he was fully aware that his wardrobe reflected that.

The couturier had promised that he would have the updates to his wardrobe within three days, which would be before he left the city. It would be of great help to his appearance of respectability when he returned to his new friends in Warwickshire, but of no help whatsoever for his appearance at Agatha Willworth's party.

He frowned at his now off-white gloves, which were beginning to fray along the seam. There was simply nothing to be done. New gloves could not be commanded within a day, not without considerable expense, and there was no one whose gloves he could respectably borrow: Colonel Willworth's gloves would be comically baggy upon Percival's hands and the query would be an embarrassment. Percival's only other significant acquaintance was with Mr. Ibrahim, whose fingers were both shorter and bulkier than Percival's, and there were few predicaments more socially humiliating—in Percival's mind—than being reduced to borrowing gloves off of one's solicitor. The old pair would have to do, being at least properly tailored and fitting attractively to his slender, long-fingered hands.

The party was already well under way when Percival descended the steps. This was intentional on his part, for he in no way wanted to be roped into the role of host for the party, and he would rather be thought vain than to endure any level of host duties with cousin Agatha's guests.

He was glad to see that both of his hosts were thoroughly engaged in conversation with a clutch of guests apiece, which would hopefully keep them engaged and leave Percival to his own devices.

The average age of the party guests was closer to his cousin's age than his own, but there were nonetheless several young ladies of marriageable age and a small handful of young men. At first Percival feared that he didn't know a single one of the guests and might after all be obliged to seek his cousin's assistance in making introductions, but then he recognised a cavalry officer whose acquaintance he was certain he had made at a gathering at Agatha's house some years before. Percival applied himself to this gentleman, whose name he only slightly misremembered, and had the good fortune to be introduced around the party from there to enough new acquaintances that he was able to avoid his cousin entirely.

Dinner proceeded pleasantly enough, and afterward the party split between dancing and the quieter drawing rooms.

Percival found himself in one of these, in a lively discussion with a group of young people who were less inclined toward dancing. He was entirely uncertain of himself while in such a group, feeling sure that his country manners should give some mis-step in the fine company of a London party.

"Mr. Valentine," said a young lady whose acquaintance Percival had made only minutes before. "Your cousin has spoken of you, to be sure."

Percival experienced a moment of dread regarding the sort of things his cousin Agatha might have said about him.

"Do I recall correctly that you are Mr. Valentine of Linston?" the young lady asked. Percival recalled that her name was Miss Josephine Martin.

"You do," Percival confirmed, uncertain about where this query was heading but indeed very much hoping that it should enable him to brag about his beloved Linston.

"I regret that I have so recently heard that name under such unpleasant circumstances!" Miss Martin remarked.

"Unpleasant circumstances!" he repeated. "My dear Miss Martin, it is my most sincere hope that Linston is not a part in anything you find unpleasant!"

"Oh, but it is!" she insisted, fanning herself and lowering her eyes to indicate her demure reluctance at being forced to present Percival with such distasteful news. "For is it not indeed Linston which has the unfortunate condition of being the current residence of Mr. and Miss Bolton of Greenwich and that dreadful Mr. Everett?"

This produced a feeling of absolute shock in Percival's breast. He did not understand how anyone at all might find the Boltons to be unpleasant and Mr. Everett to be dreadful.

"My good Miss Martin!" Percival exclaimed. "I must insist that you explain yourself! Indeed I have encountered nothing improper in the characters of the Boltons or Mr. Everett, who are, indeed, guests at Linston Grange."

"I hesitate to speak of it," Miss Martin said, and continued to fan herself. One of the other young people in their immediate vicinity expressed to her that she must be strong, and that the matter must have out.

This marshalled Miss Martin's spirits, and she resolved herself. "It is true that I have no quarrel with Mr. Bolton or Miss Bolton, other than their continued warm acquaintance with such a profligate rake as Mr. Everett, and their defence of him."

A profligate rake! Percival was quite betwattled. "Why, Miss Martin! What is it that Mr. Everett is supposed to have done?"

"I—!" Miss Martin began. She turned her face away, concealed it with her fan, and attempted to compose herself. "No! I cannot speak of the matter! It is too dreadful!"

"Miss Martin," said one of the young women seated near

to Miss Martin on the sofa. "May I divulge the matter? For, certainly, our good Mr. Valentine should know of the nature of his tenants."

"Yes," Miss Martin said. She seemed to be quite overwhelmed. "Do so."

The group immediately around them all stepped closer.

"Miss Martin is much concerned with these matters because of how Mr. Everett had been engaged to marry her, and he did subsequently compel her to break off the engagement in the most unchivalrous manner possible! Indeed, it was that scandal which caused him to depart London at once, for no hostess of good breeding would have anything to do with him, and he was turned out entirely of London society! I quite think that the Boltons will find themselves likewise ostracised on account of their having defended him!"

Percival's mouth fell open in shock. Mr. Everett, broken off an engagement? Mr. Everett unchivalrous, and banned from all civilised society? "I must beg of you to divulge the circumstances of Mr. Everett's behaviour."

"Oh, Mr. Valentine," said a young man nearby, in regretful tones. "Everyone knows."

"It was at a party," Miss Martin said. She was quite evidently upset by the matter, and seemed as though she might be on the verge of tears. "All I did—all I did!—was to ask him to dance with me! One would think that would be a small enough matter to ask of one's fiancé! And he...! He...!"

"He refused," said the young lady by Miss Martin's side.

There was a silence in the wake of this, as everyone mulled over Mr. Everett's incomprehensible and unforgivable behaviour.

"It was," continued the young lady. "It was quite loud. He said—"

"Oh!" said Miss Martin. "Oh, I shudder to remember it!"

"He said, in the rudest and most wrathful manner, 'Madam, I will not!'"

A gasp went through the assembled persons, still shocked by this unchivalrous behaviour even some weeks later.

"It was very loud," said one of the nearby gentlemen. "Nearly the whole dance heard it."

"To shout so at one's fiancée!" Miss Martin's friend exclaimed. "Why, I quite feared he might strike her!"

"And then what could I do!" exclaimed Miss Martin. "There was nothing for it but to break off the engagement at once."

"Of course you must!" chorused her friend. "How could you remain engaged to such a boor! Really, what sort of man should remonstrate with his fiancée, so loudly, and in public!"

"He was always so when he was in his cups," Miss Martin despaired. "I fear it was indicative of a dark and violent nature, but I was so determined to see the good in him!"

101

Percival regarded all of this in utter shock, incapable of formulating any sort of response. Declining to dance was all well and good, if one merely protested a headache, but to sharply and rudely refuse in such a manner while at a public party was an indication of the lowest and most dreadful sort of character. Worse so if it had been done under the influence of liquor! Percival had one or two of those in the area of Linston, who became violent and wroth when in their cups.

"You were certainly too indulgent toward him, Miss Martin." Her friend petted her soothingly. "But it has turned out all for the best. You are rid of him, and now all of London knows his nature. He will not quickly entrap another young lady into his wiles."

"I must beg of you," Miss Martin said, clasping Percival's hand, "that you will protect the young women of Linston from him! Indeed, he can seem so very charming, but I assure you that it is only a concealment of the true corruption of his nature!"

Percival struggled to put together a reply to this. There were enough persons present in support of the story that it certainly could not be doubted, and he intended to put the query to his cousin Agatha at the first opportunity so that he might be sure of it. If Mr. Everett had indeed behaved abusively toward a young lady—and his fiancée, no less!—at a party, Agatha would know the details of it. "I am most grateful to you for making me this warning, Miss Martin," he said. "And I will certainly contrive to do as you have said."

6
In Which Percival is Unsociable

Percival spent the rest of his time in London and the journey back home in a miserable haze.

His cousin Agatha had confirmed the story about the shocking behaviour of Mr. Everett. To have shouted at one's fiancée in public, especially in such a rude and callous way, was entirely unacceptable for any person of civilised behaviour, and what sort of monster could have been wroth with the sweet and gentle Miss Martin?

All of London society had cut him out. Percival wondered how he could do any different. To continue an acquaintance with Mr. Everett would be seen as tacit approval—or at least dismissal—of his brutish behaviour. And even if Percival neglected to care for the opinions of others, he himself should have moral objections to remaining friends with anyone who could treat a fellow person in such a brusque, hurtful way.

It seemed that Mr. Everett became a devil with drink. Percival didn't want to see it.

The pleasure had entirely gone out of his excursion to London. Everything had been arranged with the architect and masons, and supplies would be delivered promptly. Percival would still need to make arrangements with the quarry nearest to Linston, but that was a relatively small matter.

A few days ago, he had seen samples and proposals for designs and been delighted. Now even his pride and pleasure in Linston felt stale.

The fine new suits of clothes in his trunk had little purpose. Percival would wear them to meet with his architect and masons when they came to Linston, so that he—and Linston— should seem very fine and respectable, but there was no further pleasure in them.

He picked at the finger of his new gloves, so beautifully fitted to his hand. When he had placed the order, he had thought that Mr. Everett would find him very handsome in his new gloves and glossy Hessian boots.

Percival clenched his jaw, having no desire to spare any thought on Mr. Everett.

Linston was cloudy when he arrived. The village road seemed rougher than usual, and all the doors were shut. His beloved little village looked worn and tawdry to his eye now in comparison to the high glamour of London. A sad, muddy village, managed by a man who was not its owner. Foolish, green-horned Mr. Valentine of Linston Manor, who had believed his village to be the gem of the county and thought that Mr. Everett's nature was truly as warm as his smile.

Linston Manor did not escape the censure of his critical eye. The creamy gold stone seemed greyer than ever, and the cracks and crumbles at her edges were shoddy. What an embarrassment! And to think that he had shown off his manor proudly.

How the Boltons and Mr. Everett must have laughed at him.

Heartsore and weary, Percival descended from his carriage and made his way up the manor steps.

His housekeeper met him at the door, all smiles. "Mr. Valentine! Welcome home. I've sent Miss Smith to put the kettle on. I'll have tea and supper for you right away."

"Mr. Valentine," said his butler, bowing smartly. "Mr. and Miss Bolton left word that they wished for you to call on them as soon as you returned."

Percival fidgeted with his hat, turning it anxiously in his hands. "Did they express some manner of emergency?" Percival asked.

The butler gently took his hat from him, and then his overcoat. "No, Mr. Valentine. I believe it was a social call."

Fretting at his lip, Percival considered his options. Surely he could not continue his acquaintance with such a brute as Mr. Everett was assured to be! And yet how dreadful to refuse them, although certainly Percival could not bear to be rude about it in any manner. Countrified though he might be, Percival was determined that he should not be a brute! "Then please send a polite refusal. I do not feel at all well, and I do not believe I will feel up to calling upon them tomorrow—certainly not tonight."

"Very well, sir." The butler nodded his understanding, and went to see to his duties.

From his bedroom, where he was very soon ensconced with hot tea and a rich supper, Percival could see the glittering lights of the Grange from afar. At least eight of their windows were lit, and perhaps more. It seemed bright and extravagant, a place of charm and laughter.

"Would he truly have struck her?" Percival murmured to himself, not wishing to believe such a thing of the charming Mr. Everett.

Heart aching, Percival pulled the curtains shut.

There was nothing from the tenants of the Grange the next day, which was Monday, nor on Tuesday, most likely with respect to his claimed ill health. Percival kept himself at home and saw to his correspondence, which had piled up while he had been away in London.

On Wednesday, there was a missive from Miss Bolton, inviting him to Linston Grange the next day for tea.

Torn with guilt and anxiety at the certain insult of refusal, Percival sent a polite reply declining the invitation and claiming that he was too awfully busy with matters of the management of Linston and simply could not be drawn away from them.

On Thursday, he encountered the trio in Linston Village.

Occupied with the business of arranging the renovations and expansions of the village, Percival had gone to the village with the intent of speaking with Mrs. Peters, mother of six and most in need of some expansion to her home. Bringing along some of the samples and proposed blueprints for the new houses to be built, Percival intended to put to her the question of whether she and her children would prefer an expansion upon her current farmhouse, or if they would rather be uprooted entirely into a fine new domicile.

He had not gotten halfway through the village when he encountered the Boltons out walking with Mr. Everett. The three of them were in the company of Mr. Humphrey, the village pastor, who had Miss Bolton upon his arm. This seemed quite familiar of him, in Percival's opinion, even though he did think that Mr. Humphrey was a very charming and trustworthy gentleman who was of course entirely above reproach.

"Mr. Valentine!" Miss Bolton called, and waved.

Trapped by etiquette, there was nothing for it but that Percival should cross to them and greet them, unless he intended to give very public insult and cut them visibly in the centre of the village. Public insult was not a capability of Percival's nature.

"Good day, Miss Bolton," Percival swept off his hat in greeting. "Mr. Bolton. Mr. Humphrey. Ah, um. Mr. Everett." He fidgeted uncertainly with the hat, which he kept in his hands in the manner of a shield.

"Good day, Mr. Valentine," said Mr. Everett. "I hope your health has improved? I know that the journey from London can be a tiring one."

"Yes," Percival said, looking down at his hat rather than at Mr. Everett. "I am quite well, thank you."

"I hope you'll come soon to visit us at the Grange?" Miss Bolton expressed. "It has been so terribly lonesome without you!"

"I," Percival said, and cleared his throat nervously as he strove to find a means of polite refusal. "Perhaps, certainly," he said, and just then lost his hold on his hat due to fidgeting.

It bounced in the dirt before Percival rescued it, feeling further humiliated by the rim of dirt now clinging to his fine new hat. How foolish he had been when he bought it! He had thought of how Mr. Everett might find him charming in the latest style.

"I hope you will forgive me," Percival said, dusting fretfully at his hat and not looking at any of them. "I am expected by Mrs. Peters on some business."

"Yes, of course," Miss Bolton said.

"Mr. Valentine," said Mr. Everett.

Percival tensed, hands pausing upon his hat.

"Will you do me the honour of allowing me to escort you to Mrs. Peters?" Mr. Everett asked.

Trapped, Percival's breath quickened. "No," he said. "Thank you, I will manage. I could not possibly impose upon you in such a manner."

There was a startled silence in response to Percival's refusal.

"If you'll excuse me," Percival said, putting his still dusty hat upon his head. "Good day to you all."

He made his retreat as swiftly as he could manage, and did not look back.

Two days and another declined invitation later, and Miss Bolton turned up on his doorstep in person. She was without chaperon while calling on a gentleman in his own home, which Percival found highly unusual, even in Linston.

The butler indicated that she was waiting in the drawing room, and Percival hurried there, neatly dressed but flustered. "Miss Bolton!"

"Mr. Valentine," she said, rising to greet him. "I hope you

are well and that I have not inconvenienced you too much by dropping in on you like this."

"No, no," Percival insisted. "That's quite all right. It's all… certainly… it is always a pleasure to see you, Miss Bolton." He cleared his throat at the end of this little speech, and picked uncertainly at his gloves.

"I am sorry to be so forward, but I must ask you, Mr. Valentine. You have been avoiding us. I would know why."

"Avoiding you!" Percival responded. "No, I… I…"

"I beg of you to be honest with me, Mr. Valentine!" she exclaimed. "You have been avoiding us. Pray tell me why! Has one of our party given you some offence?"

"No," Percival said. "No, certainly! It is nothing that any of you have done to me directly."

"Indirectly, then! How have we offended?"

"It is Mr. Everett!" Percival said. "Truly, Miss Bolton, I do not know how you can associate yourself with a man of such—of such… base character!"

Miss Bolton's face went in rapid succession through shock, indignation, and determined fury. "Have you personally witnessed anything which should make you doubt Mr. Everett's character?"

Percival coloured and felt instantly foolish. "Not personally, no, but—"

"Then am I to understand that you have cut us on account

of some pernicious gossip?"

That made Percival's judgement and determination on the topic sound less honourable. He fidgeted and blustered. "I hardly judged it to be gossip, on account of how it was a first-hand reporting of Mr. Everett's shocking—"

"From Miss Martin, I warrant," Miss Bolton said, with wry disapproval.

Percival deflated, now very uncertain of his stance on the matter. "Yes. From Miss Martin."

"I don't suppose you'll listen to Mr. Everett himself, and he would indeed be quite hesitant to speak ill of Miss Martin, even now, but I hope you will consider hearing my side of the story, having been present at the event which has so defamed Mr. Everett's good character?"

"Yes," Percival said, sighing in surrender. The version of events he had encountered in London had been so broadly unanimous that he had come to assume it was the only one. "Will you sit, Miss Bolton?" he asked, indicating a chair and hoping that she would sit so that he could sit.

She did.

"Miss Martin was a friend of mine," she began, folding her hands in her lap as she related her story. "I was aware that she was headstrong and could be petty, but she was outwardly sweet and charming at all times, so I did not suspect a deeper flaw in her character. I further did not expect that Mr. Everett would be charmed by her. I suppose that since they were both headstrong people, there was some sympathy of character, and Mr. Everett found her to be appealingly sweet and gentle, so he made her an offer.

"Once they were engaged, Miss Martin spent quite a bit of time in our company—as you have done—and the four of us frequently attended the same events. It was at that point that Miss Martin's behaviour began to... alter."

Percival felt uncomfortable at this apparent defamation of Miss Martin's character, but he acknowledged that since Miss Martin had indeed defamed Mr. Everett's character, it was only appropriate that he should hear a fair rebuttal.

"I found her to be very selfish and demanding, and betimes even cruel. I do not know if Mr. Everett would agree with this estimate. Even now, I have never heard him say a word against her."

Miss Bolton looked down at her own hands, hesitating in her story. "She behaved... as though Mr. Everett was hers to command, once the engagement was set. I have certainly seen men treat women so, once an engagement is formed, which I find to be very boorish and ungentle. It was no more pleasant from Miss Martin. Around most company, she behaved as charmingly as ever. Around us, since we were their chaperons more often than not, she was only barely restrained, and often I would see her whisper something in Mr. Everett's ear only to see him colour as if with deeply injured pride. She treated him as though he were her lap-dog, and of course he could not honourably end their engagement. For weeks I found him at his wit's end, entirely miserable that the sweet, charming young lady he had sought to marry had transformed into a cruel shrew.

"Miss Martin frequently arranged that she would impose her will upon him by asking or commanding in a charming manner in public, but so as to contrive that he could not refuse her without seeming brutish. He began to avoid social functions, she began to complain publicly of his character, and at last the matter came to a head in the manner which I imagine you have heard: she commanded him to dance with her, he declined, she demanded more strongly, and Mr. Everett, at last, lost his temper and ejaculated loudly that he would not.

"The scandal of his behaviour—to so publicly cut his fiancée and over such an insignificant manner—lost him his good standing in London society, but I believe that Mr. Everett might think it worth the cost to be free of Miss Martin. We sought promptly to leave London and the scandal behind. Lord Barham was our ally in this and offered that we should reside here."

Percival sat in silence once her recounting was complete. His only doubt on the matter could be regarding Miss Bolton's word against Miss Martin's. He did not know much of Miss

Martin's character, and certainly had no skill at identifying falsity in anyone's nature.

"Miss Martin said—" Percival cleared his throat uncertainly, wishing to address the one question in his mind that Miss Bolton had not answered. "That Mr. Everett was in the habit of becoming… violent. And wrathful. When he was in his cups."

"You have not seen Mr. Everett in his cups," Miss Bolton said. "But perhaps you might be willing to judge that particular matter for yourself. I shall hold a card-party tomorrow evening, if you will consent to it, and my brother and I shall contrive to get Mr. Everett completely foxed. You may see for yourself how he behaves, and decide accordingly whose version of events you shall believe."

Percival was very certain of whose version of events he *wished* to believe, and there seemed little enough risk in Miss Bolton's proposal. If Mr. Everett became belligerent when in contact with alcohol, the situation could be easily and discreetly handled between Mr. Bolton, Percival, and the servants. And then Percival could be sure of Miss Martin and Miss Bolton's claims.

"I agree to your proposal," Percival said. "It would be my pleasure, and I confess that you were right. I suppose I did allow myself to listen to malicious gossip. If I am assured by Mr. Everett's behaviour while intoxicated, I intend to apologise most fervently to the three of you."

"I'm certain that won't be necessary," Miss Bolton said, taking Percival's hand with a smile. "We are friends again, are we not? All is forgiven."

Percival smiled, feeling much reassured.

KATHERINE MARLOWE

7
The Card-Party

Percival showed up promptly the next day, alight with pleasure at being able to return to his friends. He was sure that he had been much the fool, and that he looked forward to everything being resolved and back to normal.

The butler showed him into the drawing room, where Mr. Bolton and Mr. Everett had already begun dicing and drinking. Both of them rose to greet Percival with great cheer once he arrived.

"Mr. Valentine!" Mr. Bolton said, clasping his hand and clapping Mr. Valentine upon the shoulder. "Here you are! How we have missed you and longed for you! Is it not so, Mr. Everett?"

"Indeed it is," Mr. Everett said, warmth and joy in his eyes as he clasped Percival's hand, and then brought it to his lips to kiss. "I had begun to fear that I had given some offence. Pray tell me it is not so."

"It is not so," Percival assured him, blushing at the gallant manner in which Mr. Everett kissed his hand. It put him in mind of the conversation they had shared before Percival had left for London, and seemed to hint that Mr. Everett might wish to court him as one should court a lady. "I am very glad to be back from London and restored to your good company."

"Come," said Mr. Bolton. "Sit with us. Drink with us! Hermione has gotten us a case of very good burgundy wine."

Mr. Bolton wobbled slightly as he steered Percival over to the table, leading Percival to suspect that Miss Bolton had indeed supplied them with a case of *strong* burgundy wine.

"Will Miss Bolton not be joining us?" Percival asked, being much fain of having her reassuring and mediating presence amongst them.

"She will! She has only gone to the kitchen to see to some light refreshments being brought up to us. Have you dined already? We might certainly have the kitchen send up a meal, if you have not, or we might go down and—"

"Peace, my friend!" Percival exclaimed, laughing. "I have dined."

"And now we shall have you wined," Mr. Bolton said, pouring Percival a glass and holding it out.

Percival took it, and sampled it. "Oh! It is rather good."

"Miss Bolton has excellent taste in wines," Mr. Everett said. His eyes lingered on Percival in a fond and affectionate manner that made Percival feel warm in his heart and his cheeks.

"Here, now, Fred, whose turn is it?" Mr. Bolton asked.

Mr. Everett looked at the dice, and then at Mr. Bolton. Both of them seemed perplexed.

"Oh, dash it!" Mr. Bolton resolved. "Hermione shall be back straightaway, and Mr. Valentine is here. Let us begin at Whist."

"*Is* your name Fred?" Percival asked of Mr. Everett. He had half-formed a fancy that Mr. Everett might be the same William he had met at the Grange when he was a child—owing to how Mr. Everett's acquaintance with Lord Barham was claimed as an inherited one, and therefore one he might have had as a child. It was an idle supposition, and seemed now to have no substance to it.

"It is," Mr. Everett confirmed.

"Mr. Frederick Everett," Mr. Bolton elaborated, with a grand gesture of his hand.

Miss Bolton arrived then, and greeted Percival with happy exclamations before settling down to cards. A light repast of cold meats and cheese was shortly thereafter laid out for them on a side table, and they nibbled at the food as they played.

Percival noted that both Mr. Bolton and Miss Bolton were very attentive to see to it that Mr. Everett's glass was kept full, which Mr. Everett did not appear to notice. The entire party drank liberally enough that the general competence of their card-playing spiralled downward until only Miss Bolton seemed to be paying attention and kept having to remind the rest of them that they were still playing.

"Horatio, it is still your turn," Miss Bolton repeated.

"Here now!" Mr. Bolton objected. "It just *was* my turn."

"Certainly, three turns ago," his sister said.

Mr. Bolton scowled about this and contemplated his cards for a moment before becoming distracted by Mr. Everett, who had his elbow upon the table and his chin propped in his hand, and was gazing openly at Percival with a lopsided smile, while Percival blushed deeply and tried to make sense, once again, of the cards in his hand.

"*Mr.* Everett," said Mr. Bolton. "You oughtn't have your elbow on the table."

"Hm?" said Mr. Everett, breaking his stare at Percival and looking over at him. "That is nonsense. How am I to hold my head up if I don't put my elbow upon the table?"

"I believe that is what your neck is for," said Miss Bolton. "Horatio, for the third time, it is your turn."

"It is not!" Mr. Bolton objected. "I have only just gone!"

"You have not. You became distracted by Mr. Everett's elbow."

"I have so! And Mr. Everett, *really*, one cannot just…

just… *put one's elbows upon things.*"

In reply to this, Mr. Everett leaned over to rest his elbow upon Mr. Bolton's shoulder.

Completely perplexed, Mr. Bolton frowned at the elbow, opened his mouth, shut it again, and frowned more deeply. "Sir, I question the etiquette of your wayward elbows."

Miss Bolton took her brother's cards away from him, played the hand for him, and put them back into his hand. He did not appear to notice.

"Here, now, Hermione," said Mr. Everett, "you are cheating."

"Oh, my sweet maiden aunt," Miss Bolton exclaimed, with a deep sigh of frustration, and cast down her cards. "It is no use. Horatio is too foxed to play and you and Mr. Valentine are not far behind."

"I am perfectly capable of playing," Percival insisted. He was not sure at what point his own elbow had found its way onto the table and his chin into his hand.

"It is very sweet of you to make the continued effort, Mr. Valentine, but I must resolve that you are *not.*" Miss Bolton took his cards away from him, then Mr. Everett's from him, and began to put the pack away.

"Lo, Hermione!" Mr. Everett exclaimed. "Do not say that the evening is ended!"

"I say no such thing," Miss Bolton said. "I say only that

the card-playing is ended, and also that Mr. Valentine is most certainly not permitted to return home. I have given word to Mrs. Eddlesworth to make up the blue bedroom for him."

"Oh, I'm certain that is unnecessary, Miss Bolton!" Percival attempted to object.

"Surely instead he may share with me," Mr. Everett proposed, which caused Percival to shut his mouth and begin blushing.

"I'll say nothing as to *that*!" Miss Bolton said, but she was smiling.

"But you have not told us as to your trip to London," Mr. Bolton said, reaching for his cup of wine and finding it empty. He frowned into it. "Was it a productive journey?"

Mr. Everett reached for the bottle in order to refill it for him, only to find the bottle empty.

"It was!" Percival said, reminded of his pleasure at the prospect of the renovations to Linston, now that his spat with Mr. Everett was resolved. "Indeed, I have engaged the architect who recently designed the new village at Coxton for Lord Willowby, in addition to a skilled master mason, his apprentices, and a trio of journeymen who work with him."

Percival became distracted for some time in describing the details and plans for Linston, particularly the designs and features of which he was most proud, while Mr. Everett gazed upon him with rapturous admiration.

"How clever you are, Mr. Valentine!" Mr. Everett expressed. "You are so very—so very skilled at this sort of thing. I fear I should not at all have the head for it. How you remember such things as the location and route of the spring, in order to plan carefully around it! I should never have thought of such a thing, and it would have ended in disaster. But you! You are so very admirable, Mr. Valentine. You really are. And really *very* handsome, did you know that? You are certainly ever so handsome."

Blushing deeply at this effusive outpouring from the highly intoxicated Mr. Everett, Percival squirmed and stammered. "Am—am I? Surely, Mr. Everett, you do me too much honour—"

"Not at all!" Mr. Everett insisted. "Your ginger hair—I know it is not the fashion, but I find it so devilishly becoming, particularly on you, and the way that it waves—artlessly so! A perfect Cherubin style, although it is not at all contrived—"

"A Cherubin style?" Percival repeated. "Surely, I do not know it."

"Oh, it is all the crack in London!" Mr. Everett exclaimed. "It is the style of having the hair all over cropped, yet not too short, *fashionably* unruly—it looks best on curly or wavy hair, as yours. Longer than the Caesar, you see."

"Oh! Oh, yes, I see," said Percival, who didn't see at all, and only knew enough of the modern fashions that a man's hair *should* be cut, since the fashion of wearing a long tail in the back was now *embarrassingly* eighteenth-century, and he was simply glad that it was no longer in style to wear a heavy, scratchy wig. "Yours is also very—really thoroughly becoming to you, Mr. Everett. Why, it simply makes—"

Percival reached out, fingers twitching with the urge to brush aside a curl from Mr. Everett's forehead, but no sooner than he had done so did he remember that the Bolton siblings were still present. Feeling foolish, Percival took solace in emptying the rest of his own wine glass.

"That is so kind of you to say," said Mr. Everett, with great affection. "You are very kind! Indeed, Mr. Valentine, I like you ever so much."

Amidst a storm of blushes, it occurred to Percival that Miss Bolton's point was indeed thoroughly proven: Mr. Everett was in no way inclined to ill temperament or wrath when he was in his cups. Rather it seemed that he became effusive and affectionate.

"I like you very much as well," Percival replied to him, torn between the desire to bask in Mr. Everett's besotted flattery and the desire to hide from so much extensive praise, especially when in the presence of witnesses.

Mr. Everett seized fondly upon Percival's hand and squeezed it. "I am glad! I do indeed like you—and Linston! How charming it all is! The country—why, it's all really much pleasanter than I would have expected, and to be here in such pleasant company—"

"Oh, mercy, Mr. Everett," Percival begged of him. "You do me too much flattery, I declare!"

"I do like you," Mr. Everett repeated, and sighed.

Miss Bolton giggled. "Percival, I think perhaps you may agree with me that it is time to put our beloved Mr. Everett in his bed?"

"Oh, yes, Miss Bolton," Percival said, grateful for the suggestion.

"Will you come with me?" Mr. Everett asked.

"I will, if you will rise." Percival tugged at him.

Pacified by this promise, Mr. Everett got to his feet and immediately leaned heavily onto Percival.

"Oof!" Percival said, and laughed, getting his arm under Mr. Everett's shoulders to support him.

"I've got him!" Mr. Bolton said, and ducked under Mr. Everett's other arm. A moment later, the three of them tilted wildly to the left from Mr. Bolton's weight.

"Ah!" said Mr. Bolton apologetically, and detached. "Perhaps, indeed, I shouldn't help."

Miss Bolton had succumbed to another fit of giggles, but she helped to supervise the gentlemen as the group of them tottered up the stairs and separated to their various bedrooms. Percival went in with Mr. Everett, as he'd promised.

The bedroom was dark, with only the moonlight coming in from the window. They'd given no warning to the servants of their intention to relocate upstairs at that time, so no candle was lit.

Percival did not think he minded, and felt little inclined to summon any servant, especially when Mr. Everett was being so vocally affectionate.

"Here, Mr. Everett," he said, getting his hands inside of Mr. Everett's skin-fitted jacket so that he could slide it off of his broad shoulders. It landed over a chair, since Percival himself had only so much sense of mind remaining, and then Percival found himself pressed suddenly back against the nearest wall, and kissed.

The kiss was messy, sweet, and heated. The surprise of it took his breath away, and Percival found his hands settling on Mr. Everett's hips, pulling him a little bit closer and helping to keep him steady.

Utterly heedless of propriety, Mr. Everett's tongue breached Percival's lips, laying claim to his mouth briefly and then parting from him.

Mr. Everett did not go far, hovering in his grip so closely that their noses almost touched.

"I think, Mr. Everett," said Percival, "that we ought to put you to bed."

"You have promised to accompany me," Mr. Everett

reminded him.

"I have. And I will." Percival hugged his arms around Mr. Everett's waist, enjoying the warmth of him. "As long as nothing happens but sleep. I fear we are both hell hocus with drink, and not at all possessed of our right senses."

"I am perfectly possessed of the sense that I am most warmly fond of you," Mr. Everett said.

Percival laughed, happy and flattered, and gave him a gentle shove. "*Bed*, Mr. Everett. We may discuss our mutual fondness and what's to be done of it in the morning."

"Bed! Ah! Too cruel by far!" Mr. Everett complained, also laughing, but he did stumble toward the bed.

Percival helped him from his boots, and Mr. Everett did endeavour to help him from his coat, but only succeeded instead in pressing him down into the bed and kissing him again. It was a thoroughly distracting kiss, so that Percival became quite lost in it and only at length remembered that he should not want to sleep in coat and boots, and persuaded Mr. Everett to resume the attempt.

When they were both at last divested of their outer layers of clothes to a point that might be comfortable for sleeping, Mr. Everett tumbled back upon the mattress, one arm still around Percival's waist, and fell asleep.

Smiling at his friend, Percival laid down beside him, content to enjoy the warmth of Mr. Everett's body as he slept.

His lips still tingled from the kiss, and it was not long at all before sleep stole him away.

8
GOOD INTENTIONS POORLY EXPRESSED

Percival woke in the morning half-dressed, with Mr. Everett's warm, heavy arm slung across his belly.

This was a very unusual way to wake up, and he smiled to himself. Turning his head, Percival studied Mr. Everett's sleeping face: the dark lashes splayed across his cheek, the stern slope of his noble, Roman nose, the line of his lips slightly compressed from whatever dreams were playing within his head.

Percival reached out to brush a strand of hair from Mr. Everett's face, and then drifted his fingertips down Mr. Everett's cheekbone, thinking that he might like to kiss those lips.

Mr. Everett's eyes opened.

Startled, Percival withdrew his hand. Clearing his throat and blushing as a fit of self-doubt washed over him, Percival glanced away. "Good morning, Mr. Everett."

"Good morning," he replied, warm and playful, "Mr. Valentine."

Percival had no idea how to react to this entirely new situation, and decided that the most prudent course would be to flee at once and to contemplate the matter at length once he was safely back at home. "I, um. Shall we, ah, perhaps—ought we to go down to breakfast?"

"Certainly we may," Mr. Everett agreed, and sat up.

Percival likewise sat up, and grimaced immediately at the way the room seemed to lurch, setting up a pounding in his head.

There was a fire burning already in the grate. A servant must have come in that morning and lit it for them while they slept. This happened on a daily basis in Percival's bedroom at the Manor, and it made sense to Percival that it should happen in the grander, more luxurious residence of the Grange, but it had never before arrested his thoughts in the way that it did when he realised that the servant would have seen him in bed with Mr. Everett, even *entangled* with Mr. Everett as they slept.

Surely, he thought, this was not so very incriminating. Men shared sleeping quarters often, particularly if a house was crowded or to save money on multiple rooms. And many of those men, surely, must sprawl out their limbs occasionally over a bed-partner. Even if Percival had no personal experience as to this, he felt certain that it would be likely and that the servants might have thought nothing of it than that.

Except that he remembered talk of a perfectly comfortable blue bedchamber that had been made up for him last night and which he had not used.

He dressed himself quickly, not wanting to draw the attention of summoning a servant to help him. The boots could be got on without excess difficulty, but he required Mr. Everett's aid in getting into the very tightly-fitted coat that was fashionable, and returned the help in kind.

"What do you think," Mr. Everett asked, as he reached out to comb his fingers lightly through Percival's hair in order to neaten the sleep-rumpled waves, "are we respectable enough to appear for breakfast?"

"I think it will serve," Percival agreed, straightening Mr. Everett's neck-cloth for him. "I believe our hosts may be inclined to be forgiving."

"Mr. Valentine," Mr. Everett began, as if he intended to declare something.

Percival paused and waited for him to speak.

Cheeks coloured with a blush, Mr. Everett's blue eyes studied Percival's face until at last he stepped away without a word.

To Percival's eye, it seemed that Mr. Everett was uncertain, and perhaps even wary. It was a strange new expression upon Mr. Everett's face, and Percival did not like to see it. He found it far preferable when Mr. Everett smiled and laughed, and resolved himself to restore Mr. Everett to better humour.

"Shall we—" Percival said unsteadily, and tried again. "Shall we go down to breakfast?"

"We shall," Mr. Everett said.

The two of them nearly collided as they both made a sudden advance upon the door. Halting as quickly as they'd begun, there was a moment of awkward repositioning before Mr. Everett seized upon the door knob and held it open. Percival stepped through quickly in order that they might escape from the awkward uncertainty of the moment.

They did not converse further as they made their way along the pink and gold hallway and down the stairs to the breakfast room.

It occurred to Percival that Mr. Everett's room had been very fine. The green suite that they had given him was along the back of the house and looked out upon the Grange gardens and out across the elegantly-kept parkland of Linston Grange. From the years that Percival had spent managing and overseeing the estate for the distant Lord Barham, he knew that the green suite was one of the best, being exquisitely furnished with green and ivory wallpaper and beautifully patterned cushions and rugs. Mr. Everett's lodging within it spoke to the Boltons' high esteem and friendship toward him. Percival suspected that Miss Bolton would have the white suite—which had the best lighting and the most space and was, in Percival's opinion, best suited to the lady of the house. When Percival had been overseeing preparations for the new tenants, he had selected the white and green suites for the most detailed cleaning and preparation, expecting that Mr. Bolton would have taken the green for himself. He supposed that Mr. Bolton must prefer a cosier, less ostentatious room, and had very graciously given the best room to his guest.

Percival was still musing upon this topic when he entered the breakfast room, where Miss Bolton was already dining upon a generous repast. She brightened at the sight of her friends, and immediately begged that they should sit and join her.

"I hope that you are well after last night's festivities?" she asked, as she helped herself to some baked eggs.

"Reasonably well," Mr. Everett responded with a self-deprecating smile. "I trust that the clamouring in my head will eventually dwindle. Is that coffee?"

"Chocolate," Miss Bolton said. "Ah—Mr. Elkins? You will fetch us coffee?"

The butler assured her that the coffee was on its way from the kitchen. Percival felt no need to wait upon it, and helped himself to the drinking chocolate.

"And you, Mr. Valentine?" Miss Bolton asked. "Did you

sleep well?"

"Thank you, I did," Percival said. He glanced surreptitiously toward Mr. Everett, who was sleepily focused on buttering his toast. Blushing, Percival took a nervous sip of the drinking chocolate before realising that he ought to return the query. "And you, Miss Bolton?"

"Quite well. I am fortunate to have suffered no adverse effects from the wine."

"I am very glad for that," Percival remarked.

Mr. Everett laughed. "Do you suppose it might be attributed in any way to how very solicitous you were at filling our cups more frequently than your own?"

"Fie, Mr. Everett!" Miss Bolton laughed at the teasing. "I was being a generous hostess."

"I suspect rather you were being a conniving hostess," he chided, smiling as they bantered.

"Fiddle!" she exclaimed. "And even if I were, do you find yourself displeased by the results?"

"Certainly not," Mr. Everett allowed. "Your results are always impeccable."

"I am glad you see things my way." Miss Bolton preened, which caused Percival to laugh, and the three of them were still in fits of giggles at their own jests when Mr. Bolton joined them, groaning about having the headache.

It was not until Percival headed home after breakfast to change that he realised he had not contrived to speak to Mr. Everett about their kiss, and genuinely had no idea if Mr. Everett even remembered the drunken embrace. That, Percival supposed, would make it difficult to try and broach the subject, which was hardly a polite topic of conversation.

When Percival had been younger, the rector of the Linston parish had been a man inclined to loud and impassioned sermons on the loathsome vices of sodomy and prostitution. Percival was grateful that the parish now had the younger Mr. Humphrey, who preferred to deliver sermons on the topics of love and compassion.

As he tidied up at home and then set to his correspondence, Percival contemplated his distraction around Mr. Everett—and, in the past, other well-formed men of his own age—the kisses they had shared, and the potential risk to Percival's honour that Mr. Everett had implied at the end of the ball some weeks before. It all suggested some form of *buggery*. He didn't know how he felt about that, having always thought of buggery or sodomy—Percival was not at all certain of the distinction between these things, or if there even was one—as some unknown but unimaginable sin, in no way related to the innocent distraction he felt toward handsome men.

Wondering if that distraction itself was a sin, Percival considered inquiring of Mr. Humphrey on the topic, but quickly decided that such an inquiry would be even more impossible than conversing with Mr. Everett as to the significance of their kiss.

Percival went around in philosophical circles with himself on this topic for a bit, but found that philosophy and morality were not topics for which he had a natural propensity, and came to no resolution whatsoever.

He saw Mr. Everett again the next day in the village. Percival had been headed to Linston's general-store-cum-bookshop when he encountered Mr. Everett.

"Mr. Everett!" he called, smiling with pleasure at the sight of his friend and waving to him. "I am glad to see you. What brings you to the village?"

"Simply out for a stroll," Mr. Everett said, returning the smile. "I had thought that after strolling through the village I might ultimately call upon you at the Manor."

They paused in the middle of the road, grinning like fools at each other, until Percival realised that he had probably ought to say something, and searched for words.

"I would like that," Percival said. "If you did. Except, I suppose, here you are now, and here I am now, and, I…"

Percival was certain that there was something he had meant to say, but he lost all track of it as he gazed into Mr. Everett's kind, handsome face.

"What, then," said Mr. Everett, "brings you to Linston Village?"

"Oh!" said Percival. "I had thought to stop in at the bookshop. Well, the general store, really, though it does have books. It isn't so much like a proper London bookshop, it just—well, have you seen it?"

"I have not seen it." Mr. Everett offered his arm to Percival. "I would be delighted if you would let me escort you there. I could use a new book or two for myself."

"How fortunate!" Percival said, who was always delighted by pleasant happenstances like this one. He took Mr. Everett's arm, guiding him through the village to the little shop.

As they walked, Percival's mind kept returning to the thought of the messy, drunken kiss that they had shared. He wondered how Mr. Everett would kiss when there wasn't alcohol involved, or if Mr. Everett would ever kiss another man without substantial alcohol involved. It seemed, from his friendliness and occasional hints, that he might be so inclined, but it seemed forward for Percival to presume anything on that topic, and to be wrong would be humiliating.

Several times Percival opened his mouth to make some attempt at the subject, but he could not find the words to make it appropriate and respectable, and at last he gave up the effort and walked in silence at Mr. Everett's side.

The little shop was warm and inviting, filled with a variety of scents and spices. Jars of pickles and jellies lined shelves along the front, while the whole place was sweetly redolent with the spices which sat in little wooden kegs lined with linen. Percival did none of his own cooking and very little shopping, so his visits to the shop were always matters of indulgence and pleasure.

"Here, Mr. Everett," Percival said, drawing his attention to a little hillock of fudge prettily displayed under a glass dome. "The fudge is made locally by Mrs. Atkins, and it is sold in no less than eight shops throughout the shire, on account of its excellent quality." Percival nodded proudly, very pleased about the industry and skill of all Linston's tenants.

"Then I must try some," Mr. Everett said, with a smile, considering the amount of fudge. "And, of course, Mr. Bolton and Miss Bolton will want to sample it, as well. Let me see. I suppose—I'll take all of it. Both flavours. Minus any amount that may have been promised to other residents of the village."

"All of it!" Percival exclaimed in surprise. "Why, Mr. Everett, surely you and the Boltons cannot eat all that. You should make yourselves sick."

"No, certainly," Mr. Everett agreed. "But I did think that perhaps the servants at the Grange would be pleased by a treat."

"Oh!" Percival blinked in puzzlement, having never met a

gentleman who gave a thought to the pleasure of his servants, except perhaps on holidays. "Yes, I think they would. That is very kind of you to think of them, Mr. Everett. Perhaps I should do the same for my staff at the Manor. I am sure they would like it, particularly Mrs. Otto and her children. Perhaps I'll take them some of the stick-candy, what do you think?"

Once the matter was decided, the shopkeeper wrapped up the candy into parcels for them, and then they went to look through the books. Percival had two books which he had put on order, and the shopkeeper was happy to elaborate upon all the newest arrivals in literature that might catch their eye.

By the time they left, they each had a stack of little purchases. The shopkeeper offered to keep their packages there until a footman could be sent down from each estate to fetch them, but Mr. Everett would not hear of this, and if Mr. Everett would have none, Percival would have none, which was how he found himself headed back to Linston Manor with a stack of books that was just a bit precarious and a bundle of other little packages.

He dropped the books only once, which did them no harm but a bit of dirt on the edges, and was halfway back home when he realised that he had utterly failed to broach the topic of their kiss.

That evening he joined his friends at the Grange for dinner.

Percival ate quietly, having trouble offering or focusing on any conversation topic other than his kiss with Mr. Everett, which could certainly not be politely discussed over the dinner table.

Mr. Everett was similarly reserved, restraining himself merely to polite commentary on such topics as Mr. Bolton suggested, which were mostly lengthy discourses on hounds, horses, and hunting, topics of which Mr. Bolton never tired.

It was Miss Bolton's habit to curtail some of these discourses in her brother, at least to the degree that he would not be allowed to overwhelm the dinner conversation, but tonight both Percival and Mr. Everett were grateful for Mr. Bolton's effusiveness, and Miss Bolton herself also made few forays at conversation.

In fact, Miss Bolton herself seemed distracted. While Percival felt and Mr. Everett looked subdued, Miss Bolton appeared near to bursting with some topic of conversation which she was only with great effort keeping trapped behind her lips.

Percival's curiosity about this topic grew apace as the dinner proceeded, and by the time the port wine was served, nearly his full attention was on Miss Bolton in the hopes that she might burst forth with whatever it was that had her fidgeting in her seat and stabbing irritably at her pudding.

"Lud, I am at my wit's end!" she cried at last, casting down her spoon and interrupting her brother's recounting of a spill he had taken while hunting a year ago.

Halting at once in his story, Mr. Bolton blinked at her, being unaccustomed to such outcries from his normally staid sister. Percival and Mr. Everett were less surprised by it due to how Miss Bolton's discomfited state had become obvious over the course of the dinner, and only Mr. Bolton had failed to take note of it.

"Why, Hermione," said Mr. Bolton. "Whatever has put you in such a dudgeon?"

"It is Mr. Humphrey!" she exclaimed, and then sighed with dismal exasperation.

"Mr. Humphrey the rector?" Percival asked, very concerned that a member—no less, a leader!—within his parish should have put Miss Bolton so out of sorts. "Whatever has he done?"

"It is what he has *not* done which is the trouble," Miss Bolton said. "Some days I think—or, dare to hope—that he intends to make me an offer. But the moment I have contrived any opportunity for him to do so, where we might converse privately for a minute, he is reduced to helpless blushing and loses any capability to even converse!"

Mr. Everett laughed, and then endeavoured to cover it with

a cough. "Forgive me, Hermione. I do not mean to laugh. Surely the gentleman has some reason for his nerves."

"He may be intimidated," Mr. Bolton suggested teasingly, "or even terrified! You cannot deny that you are possessed of a headstrong nature, Hermione."

"Nor do I deny it," she said. "It does not seem to dissuade him when we are in the company of others. He has been entirely attentive—"

"Are we to understand, Hermione," Mr. Everett asked, "that you do live in hope of such an offer?"

Miss Bolton coloured and lifted her chin. "I certainly would have no objection to it! Mr. Humphrey is a very honourable man, and I am so very interested in his work with the church and the school! Oh, Horatio! I want to *stay*."

"Stay?" her brother repeated in surprise.

"Stay here. In Linston. For longer than just the summer. There is ever so much to be done, particularly with the school, and—oh, Mr. Valentine! Pray tell me that you have not yet engaged a teacher for the school?"

Taken aback by these outpourings, Percival stared at her in bafflement before he managed to reply. "A teacher? No—no, certainly. I did not even think of it while I was in London."

"Mr. Valentine," said Miss Bolton, clasping her hands in picturesque appeal. "Will you have me?"

"You?" Percival repeated, having a moment of panic that

she was referring to his offer for courtship.

"As the teacher for the school. I assure you, I am very learned on all topics relevant to a schoolroom."

"Why, Hermione!" Mr. Bolton said. "From whence has all this come?"

"You know perfectly well!" she huffed, and rounded upon him, half scolding and half pleading. In any other person it might have been pettish, but in Miss Bolton this display was a showing of intellectual and heartfelt passion. "How many years have I expressed exhaustion with the Society in London and the offers of marriage I've received from the small-minded, stuffed-up aristocrats each Season?"

All at once she deflated. The three men could only stare at her in the wake of that sudden hurricane of emotion.

"I would be glad to have you as the teacher for the school, Miss Bolton," Percival said at last. "If you are very sure it is what you want. And I am sure that, once he hears that, Mr. Humphrey will not be long about making you an offer. It is most likely that he is intimidated by such a grand and beautiful lady who might certainly expect offers of marriage from Dukes!"

Miss Bolton shook her head and smiled to herself. "I do not think I want a duke, but it is kind of you to say so, Mr. Valentine. I think, just maybe, that I would instead prefer a rector."

After dinner, the group of them retired to play at cards and chess. Miss Bolton had begun to express thoughts that she might hold another party, but had not yet resolved to begin preparations for it.

Mr. Bolton began, with very little subtlety, to make inquiries to Percival about Mr. Humphrey's character. Percival expressed his opinion that Mr. Humphrey's character—in all other matters but the absent marriage proposal—to be above reproach. These inquiries went on until Miss Bolton lost her temper and remarked to Mr. Bolton that she was a grown woman who might perfectly competently choose her own husband, and if he were to make an offer it would be no business but her own.

This kept the siblings in high temper for the evening, and they both resolved to retire early in hopes that the morning would find them in better moods.

Left to their own devices in the drawing room, Mr. Everett and Percival took up a game of chess.

"You do approve of the match, Mr. Valentine?" asked Mr. Everett.

Startled, Percival blinked at him. "What?"

"Miss Bolton and Mr. Humphrey."

"Oh! Yes. I do. I mean, she is very grand, and he is only a country rector, but if Mr. Humphrey is where she has chosen to lay her affections, I think she cannot possibly fare ill by it!"

"Are you not jealous?"

"Jealous?" Percival asked, briefly puzzled by the query until he remembered the source of it, regarding what Percival now thought of as his ill-conceived plan of courting Miss Bolton. "Oh! No, certainly not. I am not—I do not think Miss Bolton and I would be suited. I am certain that I much prefer her as a friend."

"And what of me?" Mr. Everett asked, very softly.

"You?" Percival repeated. "I suppose—oh, I don't know, I think you and Miss Bolton make for very dear friends but I am not sure that you would do well as a match."

Mr. Everett started laughing. "I meant, rather, what of your feelings for me?"

Percival's mouth fell open and stayed that way for several seconds.

Colouring deeply, he squeaked, shut his mouth, cleared his throat, and made an attempt at response in what came out at a breakneck rambling. "Oh! My—my feelings for you! Well, they are—they are—very warm, to be sure, I am ever so glad that we are friends, and—and I—of a certainty, Mr. Everett... I do find you to be *very* distracting, to be entirely honest, what with your—with your... *eyes*."

Percival gestured helplessly, attempted to regroup, and found himself only continuing to babble. "You're really—

really—I mean, I do mean to say, that—you are ever so handsome, surely no one could fail to notice as much, I am sure, and I do think, that is I have wanted to say to you, that I—that I! I find you very distracting!"

He finished this speech with a grand huff of determination, and only in the stunned silence following it realised that his declaration could not in any way be taken to be a clear expression of feelings to anyone outside of himself, and might even be taken as an insult.

Indeed, Mr. Everett made no reply, and seemed to be struggling to make sense of what Percival had said.

"That is to say," Percival resumed, "that it is not ill to be distracted by you, only that you are very likely to make a person fall out of his chair, and certainly no one else has ever so distracted me as to fall out of my chair and—and... Mr. Everett, I fear I am entirely lost in my own explanation. You are my friend. I am glad to have you as my friend, and most warmly so."

"I am glad to hear it."

"I think," Percival said, getting to his feet. "I think—I ought to return home. At least until I am better able to express myself. I hope... I hope you shall forgive me, Mr. Everett. It is late, and I think that all our tempers are on edge. It is the weather, I think! My mother always said, threat of a thunderstorm puts everyone on nettles! It will storm tonight, to be sure, and rain tomorrow, and after that everything will be sorted. So let me instead… I will hope to see you tomorrow. Will that do?"

"It will," Mr. Everett said. He took Percival's hand and lifted it to his lips, and then released it. "Tomorrow, then, Mr. Valentine."

"Tomorrow," Percival repeated, and took his leave.

9
DURING THE RAINSTORM

According to Percival's prediction, it began to storm almost as soon as he had arrived home. It rained heavily through the night and continued the next morning in dismal sheets.

He had no formal invitation to the Grange that day, and would not be expected at any particular time. As much as he longed to see Mr. Everett, there was no immediate promise or emergency which would necessitate him arriving at the Grange muddy and wet—even if he were to take the carriage for the short trip through the village, the weather was dismal and it seemed unnecessary to risk his footman and coachman catching cold in addition to himself.

Seeing Mr. Everett again could wait. Sighing as he resolved himself to this sensible decision, Percival shut himself up in his study and balanced his accounts. It was slower going than usual, because of his near-constant distraction: no matter what he tried, his thoughts persisted in returning to Mr. Everett. Mr. Everett's strong, appealing form; Mr. Everett's warm, sweet kisses; Mr. Everett's laughing eyes and clever wit.

At long last he settled the accounts to his satisfaction, but the rain would not let up and his restlessness was growing. He tried reading, to no avail, then paced along the corridors for an hour and fixed upon a leak in a lesser-used back hallway. That provided some distraction, since the butler and the footmen had to be called, and there was some debate as to the source of the leak and whether it was a flaw in the mortar or the roof.

Once the matter was settled and repairs were underway, it was still only early afternoon and Percival felt out of his canister with boredom.

He busied himself as best he could with the matters of the household, inquiring about stock and projects in the kitchens and cellars until his housekeeper and butler were both bristling with impatience and Percival got the strong idea that they would prefer if he would find some entertainment other than getting in their way and keeping them from their duties.

It had been years since he had so chafed against being kept indoors and his usual entertainments. For years he had been satisfied on rainy days with his books, his accounts, and the latest newspapers from London. Now all of those entertainments paled in contrast with a foolish yearning to see

Mr. Everett.

Half a dozen times he resolved to brave the weather, but each time he fetched coat and hat and opened the door, the storm's force seemed to redouble and he returned to his study in a fit of dejection.

Hardly touching his supper, he moped about in his study by the window and reminded himself of how silly he would look if he turned up at the Grange unexpected and covered in mud. What explanation could he give for doing so, when his only reasoning was that he was driven to distraction by a longing to see Mr. Everett?

Restless and miserable, he was alerted at last to a knocking at the front door, and sat up in shock as he wondered what emergency would bring a caller to his door after dark.

Quickly straightening his clothing, Percival got to his feet just as his butler appeared and informed him that Mr. Everett was here and awaiting him in the front parlour.

"Mr. Everett!" Percival exclaimed in shock, swiftly darting downstairs to the parlour.

Mr. Everett was indeed worse for wear from the weather. Percival crossed to him at once, worrying over Mr. Everett's damp clothing. "Oh, Mr. Everett! I did not expect you to brave the weather for me."

"I promised that I would see you today," Mr. Everett said, smiling at Percival and giving little thought to his own soggy condition.

"You shall catch your death of cold, Mr. Everett, you're quite soaked through," Percival fussed. "I would have forgiven you your promise. Oh, dear. What shall we do? I cannot lend you anything of mine, you are broader than I am in the shoulders and it would never fit. Come upstairs, at least. There's a fire lit in my study and we may set you by it."

"You are too kind, Mr. Valentine," Mr. Everett protested. He insisted that he should not catch his death, but did at least consent to be led upstairs to Percival's study which was much cosier with the lit fire.

"Perhaps if we have your coat off," Percival suggested. "We may lay it out to dry by the fire."

Mr. Everett smiled as if amused. "We may indeed. Will you help me with it?"

Percival did, drawing the coat from Mr. Everett's strong shoulders and laying it open across the back of the chair nearest to the fire. Mr. Everett removed his own waistcoat and hung it likewise, so that he was left in only his damp shirt, which clung intimately to his broad chest, and the skin-fitted breeches that showed off the powerful muscle of his thighs.

"Mr. Valentine."

Realising that he was staring, Percival snapped his attention up to Mr. Everett's face. "Mr. Everett?"

Mr. Everett took a step closer to him, eyes intent but face

otherwise unreadable. "Mr. Valentine, I... on the night of Miss Bolton's card-party, when we were both somewhat in our cups, I seem to recall that we ... kissed."

Percival flushed. "I... yes. Yes, we did."

"And it seemed to me," Mr. Everett said, taking another step toward Percival, "that you did not make any particular objection to being kissed."

"No," Percival agreed, letting his hands settle onto Mr. Everett's hips, for certainly he was very close and Percival did not think he could politely do anything else with his hands. "No objection."

Mr. Everett lifted his hand and curled it around the back of Percival's head, drawing him close and kissing him.

It was precisely what he wanted and needed. Percival didn't hesitate in the slightest before returning the kiss, pressing his body against his friend and hugging his arms around Mr. Everett's waist to keep him close.

The kiss did not last long, only a tentative exploration of each other's lips before they broke away, hesitating an inch apart.

"Perhaps," Percival suggested, "we might get you out of the rest of your wet clothing."

Mr. Everett laughed, and kissed him again. This time the kiss was more heated, both of them clinging to each other as they surrendered to their pent-up need. Percival was breathless when it broke, and he gave Mr. Everett's shirt a suggestive tug, drawing it from his waist band and letting his fingers roam boldly over the cool, wet skin beneath.

"I think," Mr. Everett said, "it might be best if we retired to your bedchamber."

"Yes." Taking his hands away, Percival let go of him and blushed, surprised at himself for having been so bold with his hands. Taking Mr. Everett's hand, Percival led him through the door that connected his study and his bedroom.

A fire had already been lit for them, warming the chill of the room. Percival drew Mr. Everett over near it and then untied Mr. Everett's neckcloth. He laid it aside and slid his hands back under Mr. Everett's shirt, drawing it up and over his head.

All of this Mr. Everett allowed with calm patience, and Percival blushed as he gazed upon Mr. Everett's naked chest. Lifting his eyes with effort to Mr. Everett's face, he found Mr. Everett watching him with a warm, affectionate smile which he could not help but return before tilting his head to take another kiss.

Mr. Everett returned his yearning and distraction, Percival was certain of it now. Their shared kisses were heated and eager, and soon Percival found Mr. Everett's hands up his shirt and pulling it off and away, exposing his skin to the cool air of the room.

As Percival's fingers pulled at the buttons of Mr. Everett's breeches, he remembered that he had meant to speak to Mr. Everett of their kiss and on the nature of their mutual distraction, but conversation on the topic now seemed so insufficient to express his feelings, and certainly of far less priority than kissing Mr. Everett. He hesitated, meeting Mr. Everett's blue eyes and wondering whether he might find words to clarify what he wanted, but then Mr. Everett kissed him again and it all slipped away from Percival's mind.

They clasped possessively to each other, and Percival could feel Mr. Everett's cool, damp skin starting to warm from the heat of the fire and their bodies.

Tugging at the laces of Mr. Everett's smallclothes, Percival pushed him back into a chair and then knelt so that he could pull off Mr. Everett's boots. Mr. Everett laughed with delight at Percival's impatience, helping to shed his clothing and then herding Percival toward the bed as he stripped off Percival's shoes, socks, and breeches, so that they were both naked as they reached the bed and tumbled onto it.

Percival's lips parted, questions caught just behind his teeth about whether Mr. Everett had done this before and what exactly it was that they were doing, but the words didn't come and instead he surged forward to pull Mr. Everett into another kiss. He felt starved for Mr. Everett's lips and tongue, dizzied by how they moved against his own and then drew away to trail kisses down his throat and chest.

Mr. Everett's tongue burned a path along his collarbone, leaving the skin tingling from heat and pleasure. Percival cried out and arched beneath him before pressing up to mimic the gesture. He tasted Mr. Everett's skin with tongue and teeth, pushing his lover down on his back as he explored the broad expanse of his chest.

Each time Percival hesitated, uncertain as to his course from here, he had only to glance up at Mr. Everett's blue eyes and nothing mattered but kissing him again. The same seemed to happen to Mr. Everett, pausing for a moment only to surge suddenly forward and kiss Percival with renewed heat. They tangled up in each other, skin to skin, and the heat of Mr. Everett's prick pressed against Percival's belly like a brand.

He couldn't resist, couldn't think of anything but pleasure, and let his hand snake down to clasp around Mr. Everett's length. It was full and heavy in his hand, the skin silken and the blood beating beneath the skin. Percival stroked it slowly, the way he would stroke his own, and Mr. Everett's hand mirrored him, clasping Percival's prick as they lay together and exchanged heated kisses.

It felt strange, and overwhelmingly good. The prick in his hand was more curved than his own, and slightly thicker. Just as fascinating was Mr. Everett's hand on his cock—the palm wider, the fingers not quite as long, the skin soft and uncallused. It felt far better than the company of his own hand when he lay alone in bed, and the kisses were exquisitely distracting. Percival kissed him again and again, laughing softly from sheer joy and pleasure in the kisses, and he spilled himself very suddenly into Mr. Everett's warm hand.

Flushed with surprise, Percival stared at him. His hand paused for a moment on Mr. Everett's length, watching wide-eyed as Mr. Everett lifted the hand to his lips and cleaned the droplets away with his tongue.

Unable to look away from Mr. Everett's entrancing eyes and Mr. Everett's soft lips, Percival resumed his stroking, listening to the way Mr. Everett's breath hitched with pleasure. He couldn't resist exploring and seeking out those reactions, finding out how Mr. Everett liked it best, and all at once Mr. Everett stifled a cry and came, spending himself over Percival's palm and belly.

Percival laughed with delight and relaxed back into the covers, watching Mr. Everett as he mimicked his lover and cleaned his hand with his mouth. Mr. Everett watched him intently as he did so, drawing a fingertip through the glistening droplets on Percival's belly until Percival caught his hand as well, leading it to his lips and hollowing his cheeks to suck the liquid away.

Mr. Everett kissed him for that, fierce and passionate. Percival hugged tight to him, not caring in the least about the stickiness of his skin. Nothing mattered but Mr. Everett, and they exchanged kiss after kiss. Eventually, the heat of their kisses slowed, both of them sleepy and warm. Percival tugged up the blankets over them both as Mr. Everett entwined their legs, hugging his arms around Percival's waist.

All tangled up with his lover, Percival closed his eyes and drifted peacefully off to sleep.

10
Mr. Everett's Departure

When Percival woke the next morning, Mr. Everett had gone.

This was extremely puzzling to Percival after the extremely pleasant and intimate evening they had spent together. He supposed that Mr. Everett might have a habit of a morning walk before breakfast, or that Mr. Everett had been called away on urgent business—although, if this were the case, Percival did not see why or how his servants might have managed to wake Mr. Everett without waking their master.

Certainly, he thought, there could be no reason for worrying. Mr. Everett was extremely honourable and kind, and there would of course be a sensible reason for his sudden disappearance.

Rising and donning his smallclothes and shirt, Percival

rang for his servant to help him into coat and boots. His valet knew nothing of the matter, but Percival's butler was able to inform him that Mr. Everett had left the manor house briefly after sunrise.

"Did he seem to be, I don't know, upset or alarmed at some urgent matter?"

"No, sir. Not that I noticed. No urgent matter was brought to the house, to be sure."

The rainstorm, at least, had passed. And taken Mr. Everett with it, evidently, rather like a spectre or a dream who faded at morning sunlight.

Percival set out without breakfast for Linston Grange. Mr. Everett would, without doubt, have an explanation for his disappearance, and he would, also without doubt, want to make that explanation to Percival as soon as possible so as to assuage any possible alarm.

The mystery only deepened as Percival arrived at the Grange. He presented himself to Mr. Elkins, the butler, and asked to see Mr. Everett.

"I am sorry, Mr. Valentine," the butler informed him, "but Mr. Everett left first thing this morning."

"Left!" Percival exclaimed. "Why, where has he gone?"

"I am not certain, sir. I believe Miss Bolton may know more."

"Then, please, may I see her at once?"

"Of course, Mr. Valentine," said Mr. Elkins, and showed him in at once to Miss Bolton in the drawing room.

Smiling at the sight of Percival, Miss Bolton got to her feet. "Mr. Valentine! I am glad to see you, and this better weather we are having today. Have you breakfasted?"

"I—I have not," Percival said, reminded that his usual routine had been thrown into disarray by Mr. Everett's disappearance. "Miss Bolton, where is Mr. Everett?"

"Mr. Everett? Why, he left this morning! Barely stopped for breakfast! Said he had some urgent business in London."

"Urgent business in London!" Percival repeated, aghast. "And he left no word?"

"None more than that! My dear Mr. Valentine, what has happened? Why are you so alarmed?"

"I..." Percival opened his mouth to reply, and then all at once realised that he had no polite explanation for his confusion and concern.

Colouring deeply, he dropped his eyes and cleared his throat, striving to invent a suitable excuse.

"Here, Mr. Valentine," Miss Bolton said. "Will you sit? I will ring for breakfast—will you have chocolate or coffee? Or brandy! It seems as though you have taken some shock."

"I suppose I have!" Percival exclaimed, and sat in stunned silence.

Miss Bolton rang for breakfast to be brought up, ordering

chocolate and coffee both to be brought with the food. Then she poured Percival a glass of brandy from a side table and put it into his hands. "Now, then. Tell me what has happened."

"Miss Bolton," Percival said, struggling to begin. He supposed that the bare truth would serve well enough. "Mr. Everett came to the manor last night. He was soaked through, but he... he had promised that he would see me, and was determined that he should make good on it, storm or no storm! I insisted that he should stay the night and be got out of his wet clothes." Blushing deeply at the memory of what had happened next, Percival drank the brandy at a gulp. "He vanished in the morning without a word to me or my staff."

"How very unusual!" she exclaimed. "That is not like him at all. Why, he said not a word to me other than his urgent business in London, but I do not see how urgent it could have been if he said nothing to you of it last night. And surely if he had received a message since then, your butler or mine should know of it!"

Upset and perplexed, Percival blinked into his empty glass. Mr. Everett, gone! Without any excuse or explanation, and no apology whatever to Percival for so rudely taking his leave.

"How—how rude and ungallant of him!" Percival exclaimed.

"I am rather inclined to agree with you!" Miss Bolton said, visibly shocked by this turn of events. "I assure you, Mr.

Valentine, I have never known him to behave in such a manner before. Surely there must be some explanation in this of which we are ignorant. Something of significance weighty enough to make him behave so! I cannot make any sense of it."

Percival felt himself at risk of becoming emotional, and strove urgently to suppress such foolish outpourings.

Miss Bolton refilled his glass. Percival drank it.

"I dread that I can!" Percival exclaimed, possibly unwisely.

Miss Bolton's eyes widened. She leaned in closer and clasped Percival's hand to reassure him. "Pray tell me, Mr. Valentine. You may be sure that I will keep any confidences you make of me."

"Miss Bolton," Percival said carefully. "Miss Bolton, would it shock you to learn that... that Mr. Everett had kissed me?"

Miss Bolton tensed very briefly, and then gave Percival's hand a sympathetic squeeze. "No. It wouldn't."

That did surprise Percival, who had thought that Miss Bolton might have suspected some warm friendship between them, but not ... not *that*.

"Oh." Percival blinked, and then inhaled sharply. "Oh! I don't suppose—he has done this before!"

"No, no! Not—no. Or if he has, and I would be very surprised of it, he has been careful to keep it from the knowledge of his friends." Miss Bolton patted Percival's hand.

"Mr. Valentine, I do know that his feelings toward you are very warm. I believe him to be fully enamoured of you. He spoke of it quite frankly with us."

"Did he!" Percival exclaimed, surprised that anyone should speak frankly of such a thing. Immediately after the initial surprise, he was seized by a powerful curiosity. "Why, what did he say?"

"He did multiple times make remarks exclaiming how very highly he esteemed you and that he wanted very much to make something of it, but he feared that you might not be receptive to such advances, even though we all thought for certain that you would be after we met you that first time and you fell out of your chair for staring at him."

"What!" Percival cried, not well-pleased to learn that his particular distraction had been so obvious.

"Oh, forgive me. I only mean—you see, Mr. Everett has spoken to us frankly before about his ... inclinations, and that has set us on the watch for any time that such inclinations might be reciprocated."

"What inclinations?" Percival asked, very surprised by all of this, especially from the well-bred Miss Bolton.

"From what Mr. Everett has told us, well, he said that he finds himself drawn to both men and women in the same sort of manner. It is not common that either should catch his eye, but I do believe it has been slightly more often that we've spotted some interest in him toward a young buck. But all of the gentlemen who have caught his eye in the past—well, they've been perfectly forward about their interest in women, and not at all inclined to fall out of their chairs for staring at him."

Percival thought it rather unkind of her to dwell upon the incident like that. "But this does not tell us where he has gone!"

"No," Miss Bolton agreed. "It does not."

Mr. Bolton stumbled through the door at that point, half yawning and half scowling. "Hermione, what in the world, I was directed up *here* for breakfast. Oh, hello, Mr. Valentine."

"Horatio, something has happened!" Miss Bolton announced.

That woke Mr. Bolton in a hurry. Blinking in confused interest, he stole a chair from the card-table and came over to join the conversation, which was further delayed by the arrival of breakfast.

None of them intended to continue the discussion in front of the servants, so they re-arranged themselves around the table. Percival found himself very hungry, and helped himself gladly.

"Now," said Mr. Bolton, as soon as the three of them were alone. "What has happened?"

"Mr. Everett," Miss Bolton explained, "has gone. He

was with Mr. Valentine last night, and then departed in the morning without a word! He said to me, since I was awake when he swept through, that he was off to London on urgent business. I didn't give it a thought until Mr. Valentine turned up in alarm to search for him."

"What!" Mr. Bolton burst out. "Why, that's not at all like Mr. Everett."

"Certainly not!" his sister agreed. "And furthermore—"

"Here, now," Mr. Bolton said, "when you say that he was *with* Mr. Valentine last night…"

Both of the siblings turned to gaze at Percival, who reddened.

"Well." Mr. Bolton grinned. "I'd say we ought to congratulate our Achilles and Patroclus, if it weren't for Achilles' sudden departure."

"Shh, Horatio, don't tease him. Poor Mr. Valentine is upset, and with good reason. Mr. Everett has behaved shockingly."

"He has indeed!" Mr. Bolton declaimed. "But I'll wager there's a reason for it. Fred wouldn't behave so harshly without impetus. You oughtn't worry, Mr. Valentine. Our Mr. Everett is entirely devoted to you."

"Devoted!" Percival repeated, blushing in startled surprise that they thought so.

"Yes, indeed!" Miss Bolton said. "More than I've seen him over anyone else in all our acquaintance with him. He was quite sick with longing for you when you were away, and when we feared that you had cut the three of us, well..."

She suddenly went silent and looked uncomfortable.

"Pray tell me, Miss Bolton," Percival pleaded.

The siblings exchanged a reluctant look.

"I suspected that you'd heard about Miss Martin," Miss Bolton explained, "which turned out to be true. Mr. Everett lived for several days in dread that you had heard some rumour of his predilections—such rumours were rare, and the betrothal stopped most of them, but... well, he feared you were disgusted with him for being in love with you."

"In love with me!" Percival repeated in shock.

Miss Bolton filled Percival's cup again with chocolate.

He picked it up and sipped at it until some of his senses returned.

Mr. Everett in love with him! His head spun with hope and with hurt confusion. "If he is in love with me, then why has he left?"

"I don't know," Miss Bolton said. Her brother likewise shook his head. "I'm sure we'll make sense of it. Mr. Everett is very deeply fond of you, of that I am sure. It was no doubt urgent business that called him away. Nothing more."

The summer filled out into long, hot days, and the fields of Linston flourished. The Boltons kept Percival company on a daily basis, playing at cards and backgammon when the weather was poor, and riding out hunting or picnicking when the weather was fine. Mr. Humphrey often joined them on their excursions, and his thoughtful moderation was a pleasant addition to the liveliness of the group.

When he wasn't immediately distracted by their company or the business of the estates, Percival spent his time gazing off in the direction of London and waiting for the return of Mr. Everett's carriage.

The trip to London would be a week in either direction, and likely at least a week in London. It was miserable weather for visiting London, and the city would be half empty. Anyone who could afford to leave London in the heat of the summer would do so, and Mr. Everett was headed in the wrong direction.

Percival replayed the memories again and again of their kisses and their shared night. Remembering was both sweet and nerve-wracking, as he continued to dread that Mr. Everett had left on account of himself.

Surely any honourable business would have allowed for a word to Percival's butler, or to the butler at the Grange—or to Miss Bolton, who he had passed in his swift departure! Any of them might have borne a reassurance to Percival. The silence Mr. Everett had left instead felt cruel and hollow.

"Mr. Valentine!" Miss Bolton called, and Percival looked

up to find that his friends had begun a game of badminton and were summoning him to join.

"Mr. Valentine!" she cried again, and waved to him.

Percival smiled, and went down to play.

His limbs felt weary, and his smiles were forced, but he did his best to conceal the aching misery that Mr. Everett had left behind.

The Bolton siblings said nothing more to him about it. Everything that could be expressed had already been said, and they simply did their best to keep him occupied and distracted. Percival was grateful for their patience and friendship. They never commented on his empty smiles and his long silences, nor did they ever draw attention to the way that he played distractedly at cards and backgammon and lost constantly.

Trying to keep himself busy, he went to visit Mrs. Hartley to check on her roof, even though the repairs had been effected weeks ago and he had heard nothing more about it in the interim.

The day was windy, tugging at his hat so that he was forced to walk with one hand on the brim of it. He walked with his eyes down the length of the road until it disappeared around a curve. If Mr. Everett came from London, he might go straight to the Grange without Percival ever catching a sight of him along the road, but that didn't matter. If Mr. Everett came to the Manor, he would come along the Linston Village road.

One day, he would return. One day, he *must* return.

Percival could see the construction carrying on in two—sometimes it was three—places at once around the village. New homes were finished and old ones were renovated every week. Percival watched their progress with pride and pleasure, and wished that Mr. Everett were here to see it. Mr. Everett had always shown such attentive interest whenever Percival spoke of the business of the village and estates.

Rapping at Mrs. Hartley's door, he heard a cheerful whoop from within.

"Just a minute, dear!" Mrs. Hartley called, and shortly afterward appeared at the door. "Mr. Valentine!"

"Mrs. Hartley," Percival said, smiling at the sight of her.

"How good it is to see you! Come in, dear. Will you have coffee? I've just been hanging this mint to dry. So much of it this year, you see! That's what happens with mint if you're not careful with it, you know. Do you have mint at the Manor, Mr. Valentine?"

"Do you know, I have no idea!" Percival replied, removing his hat before he stepped into the low-ceilinged cottage, hung all about with drying herbs from her garden. "I suppose we must—I see it often enough fresh in the summer, and I imagine Mrs. Otto would come to you for it if we had none, which you would certainly know about."

"There's sense!" Mrs. Hartley said, laughing as she put the

kettle on. "It is good to see you again, Mr. Valentine. Why, we've hardly exchanged two words since the trouble with my roof."

"I apologise for that, Mrs. Hartley," Percival said, glancing up toward the patched hole in her roof. It was securely repaired, and looked expertly done. Percival didn't know much about such things, but he nonetheless nodded approvingly, pleased that his estates looked to themselves so well with just a bit of benevolent oversight. "I shall try to come more often."

"Oh, no, no! You have your friends now, and very glad I am for it." Mrs. Hartley plopped into a chair across him while they waited for the kettle to boil. "They're such good young people, don't you think? I like them all very much. And I am so very glad to see you with friends of your own age and status. As much as I enjoy your company, Mr. Valentine, I am glad to see you kept so busy with them. You seem—brighter, when you are with them. That's my opinion, at any rate. Do you suppose they'll stay?"

"Stay?" Percival repeated. "I suppose. I think they might. Miss Bolton—had you heard?—she does seem to be very taken with Mr. Humphrey. I've told her that she may be mistress of the school, once the repairs are finished."

"Will she indeed!" Mrs. Hartley said, entirely delighted by this news. "Oh, that will be very nice. She seems to be the most wholesome and gentle young lady. I am certain that any pupils she has will only benefit from her tutelage, and we do indeed need a school in Linston again."

"I intend to have it open as soon as the harvest season is done," Percival promised her, his smile feeling more genuine in Mrs. Hartley's cheerful company.

"You don't suppose she'll find it dull? For as fine a London lady as she is, to be sure."

"I don't suppose so, no. Miss Bolton seems to have flourished in the country. Her brother may return to London, once she's settled, perhaps, and Mr. Everett..."

"Oh, yes! Mr. Everett. He's off to London, isn't he? Is it true what one hears about London in the summer? Reeks like a—"

"Mrs. Hartley!" Percival scolded, beginning to laugh. "Yes, I suppose it's true. I've never been to London in the heat of the summer."

"No, I expect not. You have better sense than that."

Percival continued laughing, feeling lighter for it. "Mrs. Hartley!"

"When will he be back, then? I do very much like Mr. Everett. Very earnest, he is, and takes a genuine interest in one! Why, he let me rattle his ear clean off about the local growing season for herbs!"

"He is..." Percival hesitated and cleared his throat. "He is very earnest, yes. I... to be quite honest, Mrs. Hartley, I am not certain if Mr. Everett will return. He departed very suddenly for London, and without proper explanation. We've had nothing from him since. Near three weeks it's been, now."

"Oh, he'll be back, to be sure," Mrs. Hartley prophesied, nodding knowledgeably. "He seemed like a country sort to me, and I can spot them."

"A country sort!" Percival repeated, not certain whether or not he ought to be offended on Mr. Everett's behalf. "Why, he isn't at all! He is very refined and fashionable."

"Oh, Mr. Valentine!" Mrs. Hartley said, laughing. "I didn't mean he was not. I am sure that Mr. Everett is the very height of the *beau monde* in London. Only, I mean—there are those sorts, whether they're born town or country, out in the country they fuss and fidget and count the days until summer is over and they may return to Town. And there are those who come to the country and they bloom and relax. No matter a person's birth or upbringing, some of us are Town, and some of us are Country. You and I, we're Country. Mr. Bolton—I think he's Town. But the other two... they'll stay, mark my words. Miss Bolton will have her country rector, and Mr. Everett won't be gone long. He's Country at heart, and his heart is here."

"I do not at all know if I believe you," Percival said, smiling hopefully. "But I like your theory very much."

It was halfway through August when Percival one day

received a brief note from Miss Bolton saying that Mr. Everett had returned and would Percival kindly join them for dinner that night or the next.

There was nothing more than that, no explanation or encouragement. Percival sent back at once that he would, and spent the rest of the day fretting and changing his mind about his wardrobe.

He did his best to wait until the indicated time before setting out for Linston Grange, but he was half-mad with yearning and impatience, and arrived more than half an hour early.

The butler met him at the door and showed him into the parlour.

It was empty, and quieter than the drawing room where he usually met with his friends. Percival fidgeted and paced until Miss Bolton appeared, alone.

"Miss Bolton!" Percival said, startled that she was alone, and not accompanied by the wayward Mr. Everett. "Why, whatever has happened? Where is Mr. Everett?"

"He's here, Mr. Valentine," she said. Her smile endeavoured to be reassuring, but there was something unhappy about it which Percival did not like at all. "He will be down shortly."

"But Miss Bolton..." Percival hesitated. He felt puzzled and betrayed by her demeanour. She knew how wrought with misery he had been in Mr. Everett's absence, but now she offered no comfort or explanation, and Mr. Everett did not even bother himself to appear! "What has he said? What explanation has he given? Why has he not come to the manor to see me?"

"Mr. Valentine," she said, appearing to struggle with what to say. "Please, come in to dinner, and do not ask me. You are both my dear friends, but I—!" Mastering herself, she took a deep breath and folded her hands. "All will be well, Mr. Valentine. I am certain of it. Please, will you come in to dinner?"

"Yes," Percival said. He was unhappy and confused, but Miss Bolton was his friend and he had no intention of pressing her for further details if she had been for some reason sworn to secrecy. Lifting his chin and straightening his spine, he followed her in to dinner.

Mr. Bolton was already waiting, and this time it was Mr. Everett who was late.

Percival rose from his seat when Mr. Everett appeared. "Mr. Everett!"

"Mr. Valentine." Mr. Everett pressed his hand politely in greeting, and then let go and took his seat. He seemed guarded and aloof, and did not meet Percival's eyes for more than an instant.

Utterly flabbergasted by this strange reception, particularly considering the context under which they had last seen each other, Percival stared at him in shock.

"Mr. Valentine," Miss Bolton said, her unhappiness only just concealed under a firm, polite exterior, "please, will you sit?"

He sat, feeling as though the world around him was reeling.

There was no conversation at all for several minutes as they all stirred unhappily at their soup.

"I hope," Percival said at last, with the same sterile politeness he would use with a stranger, "that your journey to London was a productive one, Mr. Everett?"

"Yes," said Mr. Everett. "It was."

Percival barely tasted the beautiful food in front of him. Miss Bolton made some tentative forays at conversation, inquiring with Mr. Everett about news from London. There was little enough of it—he was still unwelcome in society, and appeared to have done little other than visited his solicitor and settled some legal affairs, of which he provided no specifics.

After dinner, they retired as usual to the drawing room. Mr. Everett refused Mr. Bolton's suggestion of playing chess but consented to play cards all together.

He seemed to Percival to be very cold and very gruff, not at all the friendly and engaging Mr. Everett that he had been mere weeks ago. He replied to questions and jests only when prompted and seemed at all times deeply uncomfortable, which made the evening miserable for all four of them.

At last Miss Bolton called an end to it, dismissing herself off to bed. Mr. Bolton and Mr. Everett promptly agreed, and rose.

"Mr. Everett!" Percival said, rising also to his feet as Mr. Everett made to quit the room.

Mr. Everett paused.

"Pray, will you stay a moment?" Percival asked. "I would speak with you."

Nodding once, Mr. Everett returned to stand in front of Percival. The Boltons exited quietly.

Searching for suitable words, Percival studied Mr. Everett's blue eyes but found only cold regard in them. "Mr. Everett—have I given you some offence?"

Mr. Everett looked away guiltily. "No, not at all."

"Then perhaps you have some doubts as to my character," Percival suggested. His cheeks heated with nerves and indignation at this cold treatment from Mr. Everett.

"Nothing of the sort," Mr. Everett said firmly, and offered no further explanation.

"Then are we not friends?"

Mr. Everett hesitated. He still would not meet Percival's eyes. "Certainly we are friends, Mr. Valentine. I do enjoy your company. It is only that I have no further desire to be alone with you."

Upon that statement, he turned and left the room.

Percival stared after him with jaw agape. Mr. Everett had never before been so shockingly rude to him.

Cheeks flaming, Percival showed himself to the door.

On the way home, he allowed himself the unkind thought that perhaps Miss Martin had been right after all.

That did not, he conceded to himself, make sense with all the rest of the evidence, and there remained too many strange inconsistencies in Mr. Everett's behaviour and in the behaviour of the Boltons. But it did make him feel better to imagine himself direly wronged and to reproach Mr. Everett's character, which had now been cast into question.

11
Uncomfortable Silences

He was invited again to dinner the next day, with a polite note indicating that Mr. Humphrey would also be joining them.

Nothing had progressed in the romance between Miss Bolton and Mr. Humphrey, which had left Miss Bolton despairing whether he would ever make her an offer. Percival couldn't make sense of it, and kept resolving to see to the matter with Mr. Humphrey, but he had continually put it off due to his own troubles.

The information that Mr. Humphrey would join the party was a great relief. He was innocent of the question of Mr. Everett, and would serve as a mediating influence upon the tempers of the group.

Percival sent back a response at once, and then went out

to oversee the construction projects in progress. That kept him busy for most of the day, so that he was the last to arrive at the Grange for dinner.

Miss Bolton met him with her usual kindness and grace, and Mr. Bolton's humour seemed likewise to be restored. It was only Mr. Everett who remained peculiarly aloof. He was perfectly cordial to the company, but avoided conversation with Percival and would not look at him unless required to answer a direct query.

Percival left him alone for the most part, not wanting to make the situation worse.

"Mr. Everett," said Mr. Humphrey, who had no such compunctions and no suspicion that there even was a situation, "have you seen the improvements that are in progress around Linston? It is so very thrilling! Why, it seems like half the village is going to be expanded or improved."

"I have," Mr. Everett said, with only as much interest as was polite. "I hope it will be very good for Linston."

"I'm sure it will! The improvements to the school are being prioritised, as you may know—oh! I suppose that you don't know. They are, you see. Linston has not had a proper school in nearly a decade, but with Mr. Valentine's kind oversight we will have the schoolhouse back in repair for pupils. And, would you know, Miss Bolton has even suggested that she may wish to stay on as schoolmistress! Oh—I suppose you might already have known that."

"I did," Mr. Everett confirmed. "And I wish her the best of it. She seems to be very fond of Linston and its inhabitants."

"Indeed I am," Miss Bolton said, bestowing a smile upon Mr. Humphrey, who looked away fretfully.

An uncomfortable silence followed as everyone strove to pretend they had not noticed.

After dinner, they retired to play games again. Five made for an odd number at most of their games, but Mr. Everett protested that he would prefer not to play on the excuse of having the headache, and they were able to play more evenly with four.

Percival attempted not to watch him as they played, but his eyes kept straying toward Mr. Everett's handsome form and unreadable face.

The evening again ended sooner than had previously been their habit. Mr. Humphrey was an early riser, and when he expressed as much the party decamped.

Not wanting to linger in Mr. Everett's presence when he was so clearly unwanted, Percival left with Mr. Humphrey, intending to walk him as far as the church and the rector's cottage.

"Quite a pleasant evening," Mr. Humphrey said, as the two of them made their way down the lane.

"Yes," Percival agreed, though it was hardly heartfelt. "The

Boltons keep an excellent cook."

"Oh yes! The mutton they served tonight was unparalleled!" Mr. Humphrey sighed happily. "And it is pleasant to have Mr. Everett back, although he seemed a bit quiet tonight, don't you think?"

"Yes," Percival said. "I believe something has weighed upon his mind ever since he left so suddenly for London several weeks ago."

"How unfortunate! Has he given no intimation as what it is about?"

"None whatsoever," Percival said, since he certainly didn't intend to comment on how the matter seemed to be linked with himself in some way.

"Most likely it is financial," Mr. Humphrey said sagely. "These matters nearly always are."

"Perhaps you are right," Percival said.

The conversation lulled, until all at once Percival remembered that he had been intending for weeks to speak with Mr. Humphrey alone.

"Oh!" said Percival. "Mr. Humphrey!"

"Yes, Mr. Valentine?"

Percival toyed with his gloves and considered his approach to the matter. "If you will forgive me for prying into the matter, it had seemed—perhaps to my uninformed eye—that you might perhaps, well… that you might have some matrimonial interest as to Miss Bolton."

"Oh!" said Mr. Humphrey, and joined Percival in fidgeting.

When he did not elaborate upon the point, Percival was forced to inquire further. "May I ask whether ... that is indeed the case?"

"It is, I confess," Mr. Humphrey said miserably. "Although it is very foolish of me!"

"Why, Mr. Humphrey, why do you think so? Certainly the lady is very fond of you, and I believe that she would look warmly upon your suit."

"No, not at all, Mr. Valentine!" Mr. Humphrey exclaimed. "Indeed, how can I look for marriage in such a quarter? Miss Bolton is a lady of such esteemed quality, comfortably monied and of such impeccable beauty and character. She can expect to marry far, far higher than a village rector."

"That may be true, Mr. Humphrey, but Miss Bolton is very fond of you, and as we both know it is her heartfelt wish to stay in Linston and teach. And, as you may know, Mr. Bolton wishes to return to London at the end of the summer. Miss Bolton certainly cannot stay on in Linston without family or chaperone. If she were to marry, and I think she would indeed very much like to marry you, she could easily stay on."

"Even if a lady of quality might marry a country rector," Mr. Humphrey objected, "you must consider that there is one remaining problem, and surely no friend of Miss Bolton's could allow her to stoop so low."

"So low as a country rector!" Percival retorted, offended on Mr. Humphrey's behalf. He knew for a certainty that Mr. Humphrey was Cambridge educated and of good birth, even though he had neither land nor money aside from the rectory of Linston. "Mr. Humphrey, I think that you do yourself too much—"

"Mr. Valentine," the rector interrupted, "the Linston rectory is a *two-room cottage*."

Percival stopped short in surprise. "Oh!" he exclaimed.

Mr. Humphrey stopped likewise and turned to face him. They were still near the edge of the village, and needed not fear anyone overhearing.

"*Oh*," Percival repeated, for Miss Bolton could certainly not be expected to live in a two-room cottage. Percival knew that the rectory funds were sufficient to support the rector and his family, in addition to at least one or two servants, but it was true that the rector's house had for decades been a tiny two-room cottage near the church which was suitable only for a bachelor. "Oh, I do see the problem."

Folding his arms as he thought over possible solutions, Percival nodded to himself. "I think—with your leave, Mr. Humphrey—that I shall write to Lord Barham to inform him that our rector wishes to be married, but in order to do so he shall require larger accommodations. I am certain we can settle you with something suitable, and it is quite shocking that I have not thought to rectify this matter sooner. Please accept my apologies, Mr. Humphrey. I did not mean to keep you in a bachelor's cottage when I might perfectly sensibly have realised that you are of marrying age and temperament."

"You are too kind, Mr. Valentine! Certainly I do not wish to impose upon our landlord, and I consider myself quite fortunate in my position. But if Lord Barham were to approve the matter and … and if he were to offer some place that would be suitable for Miss Bolton—oh, Mr. Valentine! I should offer to her at once, although I do not dare to hope that she would accept my poor hand in marriage!"

"I think she should, Mr. Humphrey," Percival insisted, and resumed their course toward the church. "I shall see to it right away, I assure you."

"How good of you, Mr. Valentine. If it is not too much imposition—well, you have my utmost thanks."

On the morrow, Percival went out riding with Mr. Bolton.

Mr. Everett, Mr. Humphrey, and Miss Bolton had all begged off of the excursion, but Mr. Bolton was quite resolved that he would go, and Percival thought he should like to take the opportunity to speak alone with his friend.

Mr. Bolton was an impeccable horseman who kept a very fine seat. Percival felt as countrified as ever whenever they went riding together, but he at least had the advantage of knowing all the best routes and hidden glens around Linston.

"You have still not taken us to the old monastery that you promised us," Mr. Bolton reminded him.

"Oh! Quite right, I haven't. Forgive me, Mr. Bolton, I'd entirely forgotten."

"I do so forgive you," Mr. Bolton said, smiling kindly at his friend. "It is Mr. Everett who wanted to see it, after all, and he has been away."

"We shall go as soon as is convenient for Mr. Everett, then," Percival resolved.

"I shall propose it to him at once."

The matter was left there, since neither of them wished to further broach the complicated topic of Mr. Everett.

"Mr. Bolton," Percival said, when they'd gone not very much further. "I should tell you—I suppose I should tell Miss Bolton as well, but I do not know how to politely broach the subject. Perhaps you might mention it to her."

"Certainly, if you wish. What is the matter in question?"

"It concerns Mr. Humphrey."

"Oh, our unmarriageable Mr. Humphrey! I am near to despairing of him. Have you any sense of the matter?"

"I have indeed," Percival said. "And it was very foolish of

me not to have realised the trouble earlier. Linston's rectory is possessed of no house grander than a two-room cottage."

"Oh!" Mr. Bolton said, drawing his horse up in surprise. "A two-room cottage!"

"Our previous rector never married, you see, and preferred an ascetic existence. Previously to him, Gadswod House was part of the rectory estate, but he very generously bestowed it upon the Blackwood family, whose need was greater than his own. The trouble comes, you see, that now Mr. Humphrey is our rector, and of marrying age, and much infatuated with Miss Bolton."

"But no one could have a family in a two-room cottage!" Mr. Bolton concluded. "I see the matter entirely. Oh, Mr. Valentine. We have been a bit foolish. Poor Mr. Humphrey."

"I have resolved that I shall write to Lord Barham at once. I wish to propose that we may bestow Heatheridge House upon Mr. Humphrey. It is very nice, but it has sat empty these past few years and will need some repairs. I believe Lord Barham will be amenable to my applying some of the renovation funds to that purpose, if he will consent to me thus bestowing it."

"I am certain he will!" Mr. Bolton said. "You ought to mention the matter to Mr. Everett. I think he would find it of interest."

This seemed a peculiar statement, especially since Percival was not presently on friendly terms with Mr. Everett.

"Do you really suppose that he should?"

Mr. Bolton appeared to doubt himself. "Well, yes. I would think so. Don't you? He does take such an interest in … provincial management. And he has followed the new construction with interest."

"Has he really?" Percival asked, having not known that at all.

Mr. Bolton fidgeted uncomfortably, for no reason Percival could understand.

"Yes, to be sure," Mr. Bolton said. "We all do. At any rate, I am sure that soon Mr. Humphrey will have Heatheridge House, as you recommend, and Hermione will be entirely transported with joy."

This now settled, they rode together for a few minutes in silence. Percival had no topics to hand other than the renovations and general management of Linston, and he knew that Mr. Bolton had not the least interest in such things, despite his good manners about suffering through them when they came up.

"I don't know that Mr. Everett will speak to me," Percival said at length. "It seems that our friendship has taken a permanent blow, and I do not understand it."

"Nor do I!" Mr. Bolton exclaimed. "He is being devilish tight-lipped about it, and won't talk sense—or talk at all. I'm certain it will sort itself out, Mr. Valentine."

"You don't know?" Percival said, both stunned and relieved by this. "I thought he had taken Miss Bolton and yourself into his confidence upon his return."

"Hardly!" Mr. Bolton sighed irritably. "He made a short end to our questions and then refused to answer anything further. I do not think the trouble is you or anything you've done, and—to be quite honest—I think he's still in love with you!"

"Still in love with me!" Percival burst out, jaw hanging open in shock. "He won't be in a room alone with me! Why, I think the very sight of me is detestable to him!"

Mr. Bolton shook his head. "I don't think that's the trouble. I don't know what the trouble is, but I am certain you are quite innocent of whatever has caused it."

Percival considered that, and sighed. "That is very kind of you to say, Mr. Bolton. But I suppose I don't know what good it will do, if he still will not speak to me."

"No, nor I," Mr. Bolton agreed. "But I think I've had quite enough of it."

"What, Mr. Bolton?" Percival asked, startled by the determination in Mr. Bolton's voice. "Are you resolved upon some course?"

"I think I am," Mr. Bolton said with a secretive smile. "If Hermione and I can contrive to give you a stretch of time alone with him, do you think you can make some use of it?"

Percival's breath huffed in a surprised laugh. "What, shall I use my wiles upon him?"

"Have you any?"

"No, I fear not."

"Well, he seems charmed enough by you as you are. Can you make use of a spate with him?"

"Yes," Percival resolved, nodding once. "I would be very glad for it. Even if he will not talk to me, I would appreciate the opportunity to try."

"Then Hermione and I shall scheme, and you shall have the fruit of it. Are you free tomorrow?"

"Certainly I am."

"Good. Come riding with us. If the weather is good and Mr. Everett will go along, I think something may be arranged."

Puzzled but charmed by Mr. Bolton's playful scheming, Percival felt lighter for the rest of the ride, and hoped that perhaps Mr. Bolton's insistence might even be true: Mr. Everett might still love him.

12
The Ruined Monastery

Percival arrived the next day to find the house in a flurry of preparations for the planned excursion.

Miss Bolton answered the door, which was highly unusual, but she was all smiles and out of breath. Dressed handsomely in a fawn-coloured riding habit, she ushered Percival inside.

"Mr. Valentine! I'm glad that you've come. Horatio said that you agreed to come riding with us? We've planned an excursion—what do you think, shall we make our visit to the old monastery today? I have Mrs. Eddlesworth packing a picnic lunch for us, and poor Mr. Elkins is half run off his feet by all our requests. Be a dear and don't mention to him that I answered the door—he would be utterly humiliated, and at any rate I was just passing through the front hall. Here, come with me—"

Seizing upon Percival's hand, Miss Bolton had just started to lead him away when Mr. Everett leaned over the second-floor balustrade. "Hermione, where the devil is Mr. Elkins? Or my valet?" He seemed to be good-naturedly exasperated, and not actually out of temper, although his friendly exasperation went suddenly cold at the sight of Percival. "Oh, Mr. Valentine. Good morning."

"Good morning, Mr. Everett," Percival called politely up to him.

"Mr. Elkins was obliged to go himself to the village for preserves," Miss Bolton said, "owing to how Mrs. Eddlesworth would have them in the picnic and I have insisted that nothing is to delay our departure."

"Where, then, is my valet?" Mr. Everett groaned. "I fear our departure will be delayed, on account that I have no boots!"

That caused Miss Bolton to go into a peal of laughter. "Oh no! We shall have to have you go barefoot!"

"Hermione, had I a pillow to hand I would throw it at you," Mr. Everett threatened, which did nothing to discourage Miss Bolton's giggling.

Percival bit his lip and cleared his throat to combat laughter, charmed by the way the two of them teased each other. It was sometimes very clear that the three of them had been friends since childhood and still behaved accordingly.

"I'll find him," Miss Bolton promised, and darted off, no

longer trying to pull Percival along with her.

Left alone in the hall with Mr. Everett above stairs, Percival looked uncertainly up at him.

Mr. Everett tensed and seemed to colour. "Mr. Valentine," he said stiffly, and retreated at once into one of the rooms above stairs—most likely his own.

Coughing a few times to restore himself so that he wouldn't begin laughing, Percival pressed his lips tightly together and waited to be discovered or remembered by some member of the household.

It was Mr. Elkins who next encountered him. Returning with the preserves, Mr. Elkins almost knocked the front door into him and made a noise of horror at finding a guest waiting unattended in the front hall. "Mr. Valentine!"

Doing his best to soothe Mr. Elkins' protestations and apologies, Percival assured him that he was such a frequent and familiar guest as to be practically family—and the manager of the estate besides, and therefore should not expect the courtesy of a guest but might perfectly well let himself in. Mr. Elkins did not accept this and continued his heartfelt self-flagellation while Percival endeavoured to remind him that Mrs. Eddlesworth was waiting on those preserves.

At length, the preserves were packed, the boots were found, and everyone was saddled and ready. Mr. Humphrey was not with them, and both Miss Bolton and Mr. Bolton were too distracted with preparations to answer any of Percival's questions on the topic.

The day was very fine, with only a few faint gauzy stretches of clouds adorning the clear blue sky. Both of the Bolton siblings were in high humour, teasing constantly between themselves and their friends, until even Mr. Everett had been lured into smiles and even—once—a laugh.

Glad to see a glimpse of Mr. Everett back to his previous warm humour, and grateful to the Boltons for contriving it, Percival felt his heart swell with pleasure. Even if Mr. Everett would never be reconciled with him, Percival was glad to have made the acquaintance of the three of them, and glad that they had come to Linston to enliven his summer. The prospect of having Miss Bolton stay on as the future Mrs. Humphrey pleased him very much, and that would ensure that Mr. Bolton would return every summer with his laughter and irreverence to visit his sister in the country.

He watched Mr. Everett as they rode. Well-dressed as ever, Mr. Everett sat a fine seat on his horse, showing excellent horsemanship and a handsome profile. Mr. Everett retorted hesitantly to a few of Mr. Bolton's jests, and he glanced only occasionally toward Percival, never holding the gaze.

The trip to the old monastery was over an hour's ride, and they were well more than halfway there when Miss Bolton cried out.

"Oh!" she exclaimed, and stopped her horse.

Much alarmed, the company stopped and returned to her side at once.

"Hermione," Mr. Bolton said, deeply concerned at his sister's cry, "whatever is the matter?"

"Oh, forgive me," she said, clutching an arm around her belly. "I have suddenly—oh, I do feel rather ill."

"My dear Miss Bolton!" Mr. Everett exclaimed with concern. "We must turn around at once."

"No!" Miss Bolton insisted. "No, I won't hear of it. Mr. Everett, it has been some three months that you have wanted to see the old ruins of the monastery, and the summer may be out before you have another chance. The weather is fine, and half of the picnic is in your saddle-bags. Horatio may take me back, I will be quite well. You must go on."

Percival opened his mouth to object to this, and then realised that it was extremely likely that this was Mr. Bolton's contrivance and that Miss Bolton's sudden illness had been planned by the siblings. He shut his mouth again.

"What pleasure can we have if we know that you are ill, Miss Bolton?" Mr. Everett continued to protest, knowing nothing of such contrivances.

"Mr. Everett," Miss Bolton said. She did look a bit pale, but held her head up righteously. "You know perfectly well that I have little interest in ruins. I might easily have my picnic on any other day at any of the nearer sites that Mr. Valentine has shown us. I insist that you keep on. Pray do not argue with me further, I feel quite ill. Horatio?"

With that, she turned her horse, and Mr. Everett could not protest further without risk of making her worse or delaying her return to comfort.

They sat in silence as the Boltons began back toward Linston Grange. Mr. Everett appeared quite lost, and Percival was not sure what he might say.

At last Percival cleared his throat, fretting with the horse's reins. "Shall we, then, continue on?"

Mr. Everett's lips were half-parted, brow very slightly furrowed and eyes clouded. There was no he could politely extract himself from Percival's company. "I suppose we must. I am sure I will be scolded most fervently if I do not bring a recounting of the ruins."

"It is this way," Percival said, and resumed his course.

Mr. Everett's horse fell into step next to him and they rode in silence for some time.

Percival was the first to break the silence, drawing attention to some features of the landscape and geography of the region. This relaxed them both, and Mr. Everett asked questions and encouraged the dialogue, which soon brought Percival to smiling.

It was not much further before they arrived at the old

ruins, hidden in the cool shade of the forest. Tall trees grew all around the ruins, and within them.

"Did I tell you that this is the old monastery that used to own the Grange?" Percival asked, dismounting from his horse and looping her reins securely around a low branch. "Or, well—not the Grange, not the house, I don't mean. But the lands of the Grange, which is why, you see, it is called the Grange."

"Yes, I believe you did." Mr. Everett alighted next to him, and they walked together into the ruins.

"It used to be very grand, and very powerful," Percival said. "The monastery, that is. It owned quite a few of the lands in the region, but this was all hundreds of years ago."

"What caused it to be abandoned?"

"You know, I have no idea! I suppose I must set upon discovering that. I only know that it is abandoned—well, I suppose that's really quite clear, isn't it?" Percival laughed, setting his hand on the bark of a tree in the middle of what had once been a room. The tree stretched up for more than fifty feet into the air. "Long enough for the forest to reclaim it."

"It is lovely," Mr. Everett said, mounting up a ruined staircase to explore.

"Do be careful, Mr. Everett!" Percival cried, worried for the security of the ancient construction, which had already lost most of its roofs and upper floors, and more than half of its walls.

"I shall, I promise," Mr. Everett said, casting a warm smile in Percival's direction.

It put Percival in mind of the last time that Mr. Everett had climbed up a ruined staircase and smiled at him, and Percival stopped where he was, frozen with want, hurt, and confusion.

Goaded to some action by a sudden rush of indignation, Percival made his way to the bottom of the steps and then paused again in a fit of indecision. "*Mr. Everett*," he called.

Mr. Everett appeared around the bend in the wall and looked at Percival in puzzlement. "Mr. Valentine?"

"Mr. Everett, I think you have behaved *abominably*," Percival said, feeling all his pent-up frustration bubbling up inside of his wounded heart.

Mr. Everett's lips parted in surprise and he descended a single step. "Mr. Valentine."

"Not a word! Not a word did you say to me when you left," Percival continued. "I was left half in a panic. And then you returned, and still you will not offer any explanation. You treat me coldly but you insist that I have given no offence. You say we are friends, but you will not speak to me. To be quite earnest, Mr. Everett, I begin to suspect whether you are the sort of rake who, once your conquest has been had, you lose all interest in the game!"

Mr. Everett's jaw fell fully open in shock. "Mr.

Valentine!"

"My name," Percival said, having worked himself fully into a temper, "is *Percival,* and I would thank you to use it!"

Mr. Everett shut his mouth again. Percival thought that he saw Mr. Everett's lips twitch slightly with a smile.

"Percival," Mr. Everett repeated, descending a few steps further. "I quite like that name. Mine is William."

Now it was Percival's turn to be confused. "It isn't!" he objected, his temper now not quite sure of its proper outlet. "Your name is Frederick. I have heard Mr. Bolton call you so."

"My name," Mr. Everett said, descending two more steps, "is William Frederick—"

He paused, still three steps above Percival.

"Barham," Mr. Everett finished, very quietly, with his eyes on Percival's face. "Fourth Marquess of Linston."

Percival stared at him, deeply uncertain.

"Everett was my mother's maiden name," he continued. "I've gone by it in London for most of my life, having little wish to associate myself with the old man. Only a few of my closest friends—and my solicitor—ever knew."

"My Lord Barham," Percival said, feeling confused and betrayed. "You've made a fool of me."

Mr. Everett—*William*—Lord Barham descended the last steps to stand in front of Percival. "That wasn't my intention.

I wanted—especially after I met you, I wanted to befriend you as an equal, not as your landlord."

"You are not my landlord," Percival pointed out. "You may be the Marquess of Linston Grange and the village, but I have the Manor *entirely* in my own right."

Lord Barham's lips twitched again. "I know that, Percival. I didn't mean—I simply meant that I wanted to be your friend. I've been plain Mr. Everett for most of my life. I don't want to be Lord Barham."

"And yet you are," Percival said.

"And yet I am. If it doesn't make you wroth, I intend to stay on at the Grange. London doesn't suit me. It never has, but I never expected to love the country as I do. I want to stay. I want to be a part of your life. I want to work together with you to manage the estates that you love so much."

"You *don't*," Percival said pettishly. "Or, if you will, I won't have you. You have acted cruelly toward me, and you will not tell me why!"

Lord Barham winced. "Percival…"

"Have it out!" Percival demanded, clenching his fists with hurt fury. "Why did you bed me and then leave me? *Why?*"

"Percival," Lord Barham repeated.

"I have changed my mind!" Percival burst out, entirely trembling with the force of his tangled emotions. "You may not call me Percival. Not if you're… not if you're…"

Percival deflated all at once. "Not if you don't love me."

Lord Barham sat down upon the steps, resting his arms upon his knees. When Percival glanced up at him, Lord Barham looked away.

"*Why?*" Percival repeated.

"Percival, I pray you—a moment to collect my thoughts. Please."

Subsiding, Percival frowned down at the stone steps between them.

Lord Barham held his hat in his hands, fretting nervously at the brim. "I'm terrified."

That was the last thing Percival expected from him, and his head came up swiftly. "Terrified!"

"*Percy.*"

Percival subsided again to let him finish. Crossing his arms petulantly, Percival considered whether or not he liked being called Percy, which no one had done since he was a child, and supposed that it might be allowed, *if* Lord Barham loved him, which he certainly hadn't said that he did, but he had nonetheless familiarly continued calling him Percival.

"I keep thinking," Lord Barham said, very quietly, "that you will behave as Josephine did. Even though I know that is foolish."

"*Josephine,*" Percival repeated, wanting to know who Josephine was and what she had to do with anything. "Who in the world is—oh! Miss Josephine Martin."

"Yes."

Lord Barham did not elaborate further.

Percival bristled. "What in the world can you mean by that!"

"I let myself love her," Lord Barham tried to explain. "And as soon as I did, she turned entirely from being charming and became cruel and demanding. She had laid a net for me, because she knew I had a fortune—even though she didn't know about the title. Once she had me affianced, she treated me like a pet, and I could not honourably rescind my offer. I keep dreading that you will do the same."

"*We* are not going to be engaged," Percival pointed out, still feeling entirely prickly.

Lord Barham laughed softly, glancing up. "No, I suppose we're not, are we? That isn't much done."

"I require no contract or engagement of you. Our relationship, such as it is or might be, is purely sociable and at-will. It might be broken off as easily as any friendship."

"That's true," Lord Barham said, rising to his feet and descending the steps. "I am deeply sorry, Percival. I panicked. And each time I thought of coming back here and facing you, I panicked again. I couldn't bear to be away from you, and I missed you achingly for every day that I was gone, but once I'd returned I couldn't manage to look at you without feeling a rush of terror that you should break my heart the way Josephine did."

He stopped in front of Percival, hat in hand, and then turned to set his hat upon a low stone wall so that he could instead take Percival's hands into his own. "I have behaved abominably, and I will understand if you cannot forgive me. I did not see—I did not think of what misery I had put you through until just now when you accused me of being cruel and I realised what my cowardice had inflicted upon you. I'm an utter fool, Percy, and I hurt you."

"Yes," Percival confirmed, but he continued letting William hold his hands. "You did."

"Are we still friends?" William asked.

Percival licked his lips and then nodded. "Yes. We never ceased being friends."

"And will you…" William hesitated, taking a breath. "I'm so sorry, Percival—even now I can hardly order my thoughts out of the misguided dread that you will break my heart and toy cruelly with it."

"I won't," Percival said, and scowled.

"Then will you let me court you?" William asked, giving Percival's hands a warm squeeze.

"Yes," Percival decided. "If you'll promise… well, if you'll try very hard not to panic and dart off without a word again. I hope you might trust me that I am not a cruel person, and I would never toy with you in such a way."

"I know," William said, and kissed him.

13
Lord Barham of Linston Grange

The forest was cool and quiet around them, and the ancient stones of the monastery provided them all the privacy they needed as they kissed. Percival hugged his arms tight around William, keeping him close and kissing him again and again until they were both dizzy and smiling with pleasure.

When at last the kiss broke, Percival gazed at him in silence, studying William's kind blue eyes and the sweet, happy smile on his lips. Heart pounding against his ribs, Percival couldn't manage any words at all, and could barely manage any thought but longing for his William.

Gently, William nudged him toward the steps so that they both could sit. Percival leaned back against the wall that flanked one side of the ruined stairs, and let his long legs dangle over the far side, while William sat a step beneath him and leaned back against Percival's thigh. They sat in silence, both of them recovering from their emotions and the strain of being apart and hurt for so long.

Percival's hand toyed gently with William's hair until William caught that hand and kissed it, keeping possession of it and holding it against his heart.

"I love you," William said, looking up over his shoulder.

Percival blushed and smiled, leaning forward to wrap an arm around William's shoulders and pressing his face into William's hair. "I…" he said, uncertain for a moment because he had never put a word to his feelings but 'distraction'.

He knew now that this was so much more than mere distraction. He longed for William, had thought of William constantly since the day they met. When William gazed upon him, Percival felt like more than just a provincial country oaf. William made him feel like his babbling about crop yields and cottage construction was valuable and fascinating.

"I love you," Percival whispered against his ear, tightening his arms around William's shoulders and hiding his face shyly in his lover's hair.

William laughed happily and turned, pressing himself up so that he could take a kiss from Percival's lips.

Blushing and grinning so much that he thought he would never stop, Percival cupped his hand around William's jaw, returning each sweet, chaste, lingering kiss until he couldn't resist any longer and slipped his tongue into William's mouth, pouring all his need and affection into the kiss until they were both nearly vertical upon the steps and panting with desire.

William's cheeks were also painted with a blush, and Percival ran a fingertip along the crest of his lover's cheekbone, admiring it.

"We should return to the Grange and inform the others that we've made up," William suggested, but he made no effort to untangle himself from Percival.

"Have we made up?" Percival asked. "I'm still terrified that if I let you up you'll dart off again."

William glanced away guiltily, arms hugging tighter around Percival's waist. "I shan't, Percival. I—as I told you, I live in dread that I will be hurt again, but ... you are so different from her. *This* is so different. And I cannot deny any longer that I have lost my heart to you. It is in your possession completely. I am devoted to you. Even if you do one day break my heart— though I do not believe that you ever could—I would rather risk devastation than live without you. I love you, Percival."

Lifting his head, William smiled shyly at him, and Percival hugged him close in return.

"I love you," Percival said, heart bubbling with affection and need. "I love you."

They clung to each other for some time more, slowly relaxing into trust for their new promises.

Percival drifted his fingertips lazily along William's arm. "Are you hungry? We have that picnic, or at least some assorted parts from it."

William smiled and nodded. "I'll fetch it."

Watching him fondly as he rose, Percival stayed where he was. The stones were cool and smooth against his back, and the sun shone down motley through the green leaves, casting patterns of sun and shadow upon William's fine form and well-fashioned coat.

"Ah, how convenient is this!" William exclaimed, as he drew forth the neatly-wrapped packages that had been tucked into his saddlebags. He brought them over and laid them on the steps. "It seems we have two napkins, two sets of silver, and even two cups. What a remarkable coincidence." Smirking wryly, he glanced up at Percival. "I suspect some manner of contrivance."

Starting to laugh, Percival pressed the back of his hand to his lips and tried to contain his giggles. "There may have been some contrivance."

"And I suppose that we'll return to the Grange to find Hermione miraculously cured and perfectly lively once again?"

"That does seem the most likely possibility," Percival agreed, holding the cups as William poured the wine.

"I am befriended of a pack of manipulative schemers,"

William lamented.

"That seems very fortunate for you."

William laughed, and leaned up to kiss him again. "It is. It seems to have won me the heart of the man I love."

They dined in a leisurely manner, feeding each other morsels of fruit and cheese between kisses and blushing, lingering glances. Percival found that William stayed constantly in physical contact with him, resting his arm upon Percival's thigh and brushing his thumb along the fabric of his breeches.

"Lord William Frederick Barham," Percival murmured, once they'd devastated most of their picnic and were sitting together in sleepy satiation. "Fourth Marquess of Linston."

William gave a little hum of confirmation.

Re-evaluating everything he knew, Percival leafed his fingers through William's hair. "Are you the boy I met as a child?"

"What?" William lifted his head and gave him a puzzled look.

"You must have spent some time at the manor as a child. I remember it being occupied by Lord Barham, your father. I was very young, and I hardly remember it, except for one party at the Grange where I was pulled all about by an adventurous young boy named William."

William sat up and stared at him. "Good lord! You're the little ginger-haired boy!"

"So it was you!"

"It was me," William confirmed, laughing. He reached up to comb his fingers through Percival's hair. "Your hair is darker than it was then. I remember it being just the edge between blond and a shocking orange. It has darkened very prettily into a sandy red."

"I am glad my hair made such an impression upon you," Percival said, laughing. "I cannot believe you called it shocking."

"It was very bright. You were like a little torch at the party."

"You kissed me," Percival said.

William looked very briefly startled, and then smiled impishly. "I do believe that I did. It seems to be rather a habit of mine."

Percival laughed, and leaned down to kiss him once again.

The day was half gone by the time that they finally parted long enough to pack up their picnic and mount upon their horses. They rode side by side back toward the Grange, keeping their horses at a walk because neither of them wanted to part each other's company or to end the sweet intimacy of their afternoon any sooner than necessary.

"I shall feel rather guilty if Hermione is indeed feeling ill," William commented.

Percival laughed in surprise and blushed. "Oh, to be sure, if she is feeling poorly, I am sure that Mr. Humphrey has found his way to her side and is nursing her most attentively. Oh, no! Mr. Humphrey!"

Alarmed at this sudden outburst, William drew his horse up and appeared concerned. "What is it? What is the matter with Mr. Humphrey!"

"Oh, oh! No, forgive me, Mr.—William. I have just realised several things at once. We have discovered what the trouble is with Mr. Humphrey's lack of proposals, and it has just now become clear to me why Mr. Bolton suggested that I should bring the matter to your attention when I said I should write to Lord Barham."

"Ah," William said, relaxing again and nudging his horse to resume walking. "I am sorry about that, I know it was a bit silly that you kept having to send to London when I was perfectly well right here. I did my best to pre-empt your letters to my solicitor, when I could."

"So that is how he sent back so quickly with the approval for the construction! And with the increased budget!"

"Yes. I do apologise for the deception, Percival."

"I don't mind. Not now that I know you are my Lord Barham."

"I am very specifically *your* Lord Barham, but preferably more often your loyal and loving William. Now what's this about Mr. Humphrey?"

"The parish rectory bestows him with only a two-room cottage," Percival began.

He laid out the entire matter in detail for William's approval the way he had done for Horatio, explaining how the previous rector had not needed a larger residence, but now that Mr. Humphrey was of age and disposition to be married, a proper residence was required.

"Heatheridge House," William repeated, when Percival had finished explaining the circumstances. "I am not familiar with it. You think it will be suitable?"

"It needs some repairs, but there is money that can be applied to that, and both Mr. Humphrey and Miss Bolton are very fond of that sort of project. I think it would suit them exceedingly well."

"Then they shall have it," William approved, holding his head up like the generous and noble lord of the land that he was.

"They shall be ever so happy to hear of this," Percival said, reaching over to clasp William's hand. William squeezed it, and gave him a besotted smile.

When they returned to the Grange, they found that Miss Bolton had indeed made a remarkable recovery, and was feeling well enough to sit up and play cards with Mr. Humphrey, while

Mr. Bolton sat nearby with a book and chaperoned.

"Mr. Humphrey," William said, as they entered the room. "The very man I wanted to see."

"Mr. Everett!" Mr. Humphrey said, rising to his feet. "I am sure you do me too much honour. What may I do for you?"

"If it please you, Mr. Humphrey," William said, "first may I explain that Everett is my mother's maiden name, which I have used for some years."

Grinning hugely, Mr. Bolton tossed aside his book and got to his feet. "Oh, pray let me make the formal introductions. I take it that Mr. Valentine knows already?"

"He does," William said, nodding his permission.

"Mr. Humphrey," Mr. Bolton said, bowing elegantly. "May I introduce to you Lord William Barham, Fourth Marquess of Linston. My Lord Barham, Mr. Humphrey, the very respectable rector of Linston parish."

William also made a good-natured bow to the astonished Mr. Humphrey. "A pleasure to formally make your acquaintance, Mr. Humphrey. I apologise for any deception."

"Why, how is this?" Mr. Humphrey asked, amazed by the revelation.

"A long and personal story, if you will excuse it," said William. "Suffice it to say that I am Lord Barham, and it has today been brought to my attention that the kind generosity of your predecessor has left you in a difficult position. It is my strong opinion that the rector of Linston parish ought to be housed as fits a gentleman and a man of the church, and as such I immediately bestow upon you Heatheridge House, to be held in perpetuity as a part of the rectory of Linston parish."

Mr. Humphrey gave a cry of amazement. "Mr. Ev—My good Lord Barham! Heatheridge House! Is this truly—oh! How good of you!"

"Isn't that the pretty little two-storey house that we rode by some weeks ago, Mr. Valentine?" Miss Bolton asked.

"It is," Percival confirmed. "It will need some repairs, but I've set aside the funds for that and scheduled it in with the other renovations being enacted in Linston."

Miss Bolton blushed and beamed. "What a lovely place it was. I do think it would be a splendid sort of place to raise a family."

"Oh, Miss Bolton!" exclaimed Mr. Humphrey.

Mr. Bolton strode forward and clasped the elbows of his male friends. "Mr. Valentine, Lord Barham, won't you come with me? I've been meaning to show you some item of interest in the gallery. I think that perhaps Mr. Valentine might be able to elaborate upon its history."

The three of them left quickly. When Percival glanced back, he saw Miss Bolton and Mr. Humphrey gazing at each other with rapt faces, already oblivious to their departing friends.

It was scarcely ten minutes later that Mr. Humphrey and Miss Bolton burst in upon them in the gallery, beaming excitedly and clasping hands.

"Horatio!" Miss Bolton said, "Fred—er, *William*, is it now? And Mr. Valentine. Mr. Humphrey has proposed!"

"Congratulations!" William exclaimed.

"Ah, what a surprise!" Mr. Bolton teased. "I don't suppose we ever would have expected such an occurrence."

"I hope you approve, Mr. Bolton," Mr. Humphrey said.

"Of course I approve. I am entirely confident that my sister is in good hands, and I think she shall have everything that her heart desires: her Mr. Humphrey, her pretty country house, and the teaching position at Linston school. Are you happy, Hermione?"

"Blissfully, Horatio," she said, and kissed her brother's cheek.

"Then I think we ought to celebrate," Mr. Bolton said. "And you, William, are you and Mr. Valentine on civil terms once again?"

"More than civil," William confirmed, taking Percival's hands. "We are the dearest of friends once again, and expect to remain so."

"Then I shall call for a bottle of champagne wine from the cellar, and we shall drink to it." Mr. Bolton declared, and went to ring for a servant.

"My Lord Barham," Mr. Humphrey asked. "Am I to understand that you might continue your residence here at Linston Grange?"

"I shall indeed," William said. "You must forgive me for my little deception—the Boltons have never been my tenants. They have always been my guests; and my allies, in regards to some embarrassment I suffered in London and sought to escape. We came only for the summer, but I now intend to stay on a permanent basis. I will be the Marquess of Linston in duty as well as name, and I shall trust eternally to Mr. Valentine's impeccable judgement in the management of the estates."

When their friends had all retired for the evening, William and Percival made their way upstairs to William's bedchamber.

"How strange to think of all this as yours!" Percival said, going to the window to watch the last evening light fading over the park and forest lands surrounding the Grange.

"Ours," William corrected, coming over to put his arms around Percival's waist. "As you perfectly well know. A portion of the Linston estates are yours in your own right, and I certainly cannot be trusted to manage mine without your guidance and wisdom."

"Ours," Percival repeated, having a difficult time accepting that concept in his own mind. A partnership with William, in both love and business. "This is more than I ever dreamed of."

"It is different than I ever dreamed. I was always dreaming of exotic adventures, trying to get as far from England as I could. I never imagined that my heart was always here waiting for me."

"Why did you leave, if I may ask?"

"My father found out that I had ... inclinations toward my own gender. I have inclinations toward women, as well, but it is not so strong, and my affections toward anyone else have certainly never been to the intense degree that they are with you. I think I was only charmed by Miss Martin, but I didn't know the difference. I love you, Percival. Hopelessly."

Percival laughed and kissed him, pulling back after a minute to study William's eyes. "You got distracted from my question."

"What was your question?"

"Why did you leave?"

"I left as soon as I could. My father was domineering and judgemental. He suspected me constantly of indiscretion—often correctly—and sent me to the strictest of boarding schools in hopes that my passionate nature might be ground out of me."

Percival raised his brows. "Should I be concerned for

indiscretions?"

"No," William promised him, and stole another kiss. "I am passionate but loyal. Each of my indiscretions—well, I was always passionately loyal to them, and it always ended poorly. But I think that a part of me was always thinking of a sweet-natured ginger-haired boy who had once giggled when I kissed him."

"I did not," Percival objected, and then laughed as William swiftly pounced him in a kiss for it.

They ended up on the bed, tangled in each other's arms and gazing into each other's eyes.

"I love you," said William, combing his fingers through Percival's hair. "I love you, and Linston, and I vow that I shall always do my best by you both."

"And I love you," Percival murmured, leaning in to take a soft kiss from his lover's lips. "My Lord Barham."

"Mr. Valentine."

Percival laughed and kissed him again. "William."

"Percy," William said, and silenced him properly with a deep, lingering kiss.

About the Author

Katherine Marlowe has a history degree, specializing in LGBTQA+ history, and she can very easily be distracted into lengthy discussions on queer cultures and subcultures in dozens of different historical eras and subcultures. When she isn't writing novels and novellas about handsome men smooching and living happily ever after, she is usually baking, hiking, or fighting eldritch deities in Arkham.

Thanks for reading! If you enjoyed the book please consider leaving me a review! I'd love to hear from you.

katherinemarlowe.wordpress.com

kittymarlowewrites@gmail.com

Chapter 1
A Visit from Mr. Sutton

Once it was put on paper, the list of people to whom Algernon Clarke owed money was much, much lengthier than the list of people who owed money to him. He frowned at this list and strained his mind to remember some source of funds which he might have forgotten, but only succeeded at remembering another two names of his debtors.

On the right half of the paper, the five gentlemen who owed him money were all friends of his who were excellent company at drinking or gambling, but not much in the habit of repaying debts.

Worse, then, was the left half of the paper, which contained a detailed list of the debts Algernon owed which would soon come due: landlord, public house tab, three creditors who had not been satisfied with the seizure of his townhouse, the former staff of the townhouse who had not been paid when the creditors seized his other assets, the stables where he had kept his horse while he still had one, and Algernon's fellow investors in the steamship venture. He didn't even properly owe any money to the last, and was as much a victim as any of them, but the other investors had universally gotten it into their heads that Algernon, being the primary investor and most enthusiastically dedicated to the research of the proposed new engine, had some idea where the project management had absconded.

It had really been a thrilling project, such as would make faster, more elegant steamships, but the leads and inventors behind the project had made a sudden disappearance, and Algernon was sunk.

He reached for the bottle of gin sitting on the desk only to find it empty. Grimacing, Algernon peered into the bottle as though some droplets might be resisting gravity but yet might be spied out by the naked eye. This did not turn out to be the case.

Taking up his quill again, he considered the lists once again. Even if his friends were all to suddenly make good upon their debts, the amounts would not be enough to chase off all the rest of the debtors.

It further occurred to him that he did have some similar debts to friends, small matters incurred over cards or capital lent for some small venture, but those seemed like unimportant and entirely forgivable debts, so he decided it was unnecessary to add them to the list.

Recognising Mr. Cullen's step upon the stair, Algernon flipped over the incriminating page and put on a dashing smile which he hoped would convey that their straits were really not entirely dire and they probably had at least a week before the creditors took legal action to confine him to a debtor's prison.

His long suffering valet, Mr. Cullen, had seen this smile before. It gave him pause as he opened the door to their cramped little garret room, and his eyes narrowed suspiciously at Algernon.

"Cullen! You've returned," Algernon said, persisting with the smile in hopes that increasing its intensity might achieve the desired result. "I don't suppose you brought anything to drink?"

"I most certainly have not," Mr. Cullen said, handing Algernon a package which revealed nothing but stale bread and slightly-moldy cheese. Algernon wrinkled his nose at it, then remembered that he ought to be grateful and quickly hid the expression. Mr. Cullen broke both bread and cheese, taking half of each for himself. Algernon noted that Mr. Cullen selflessly took the slightly smaller, slightly moldier halves of each.

Frowning dismally at his meal, Algernon poked at it, and

resolved to eat it only because he wasn't entirely certain when he had otherwise last eaten. He did wish that there was some gin to wash it down, if only because the bread was really very dry.

"I did not think you would come back," Algernon admitted, as he nibbled at the food. His stomach growled and clenched, and he thought wistfully of veal pies and strawberry jellies.

"I'm insulted that you would question my loyalty," Mr. Cullen huffed. He was an earnest, good-hearted gentleman who had served Algernon as a valet for nearly a decade, and had categorically refused to abandon Algernon even in their current drastic circumstances.

"You ought not to have come back," Algernon said, trying to be reasonable. "You could certainly fetch a respectable position in a good household, and I would be pleased to recommend you. I am three months in arrears on your pay, Cullen, and it is your meagre savings that has been feeding us both."

"I won't abandon you," Mr. Cullen said obstinately.

"Not until I'm off to the debtor's prison? Or do you intend to follow me even then?"

Mr. Cullen shifted uncomfortably. "Until then," he said quietly, not denying that Algernon would be bound there within a fortnight.

Algernon reached again for the bottle of gin. It was still

empty.

Footsteps on the stairs below caught at his attention, but he gave no particular thought to them until they climbed flight after flight of the creaking wooden steps. As they mounted the final steps to the garret room at the top, Mr. Cullen rose to his feet.

"Cullen," Algernon started to object, "I really don't think that—"

Mr. Cullen glanced back at him, the very picture of a respectable valet, and Algernon sighed guiltily. If Mr. Cullen was going to insist on remaining with him out of loyalty and friendship, Algernon thought it was excessive of him to continue serving as a valet as though Algernon was still a respectable gentleman. That argument had already been had repeatedly, to no avail.

The visitor outside rapped at the door, and Mr. Cullen opened it, and bowed. "Sir."

On the opposite side of the door was a stout man of intermediate age with a very lofty top hat. He gazed up at the tall and very formal Mr. Cullen with puzzlement, then past him to where Algernon was seated rakishly upon the desk chair. The stranger cleared his throat, clearly at a loss for words for a garret room equipped with its own valet-cum-butler.

Mr. Cullen had no salver to offer, so he extended his hand, palm up, in expectation of the visitor's calling card.

This only seemed to further fluster their visitor, who bristled indignantly.

Algernon coughed to cover his laugh, and got to his feet, cutting through the confused formality of the scene at once. "Come now. I imagine you're looking for me. Tell us your business."

"Are you Mr. Algernon Clarke?"

"I am," Algernon said, although he expected this visit to involve a court summons or a warrant.

The stout man upon the threshold turned his attention more fully upon Algernon and startled again, sputtering briefly.

That was a familiar response, though tiresome. It had become customary for strangers, upon meeting the gentleman bearing the respectable English name of Algernon Clarke, to react with surprise at finding him to be a very handsome and tall young gentleman who was, in fact, only half English. Algernon himself thought that his dark eyes and warm complexion, inherited from his mother's people in India, made him very strikingly attractive, but he was accustomed to receiving very different reactions from small-minded Englishfolk, especially the ones who had him at a financial disadvantage.

Algernon resumed his dashing smile, not intending to offer any assistance in the matter of his colour, and waiting for the inevitable comment upon it.

Flushing deeply, the stranger cleared his throat again and lifted his chin. "Mr. Clarke," he said, and doffed his hat, clasping it in his hands. "What a very great pleasure to make your acquaintance."

This was not at all the reaction that Algernon had expected, and he exchanged a startled glance with Mr. Cullen.

"I," continued their visitor, "am Mr. Sutton, Esquire." He offered his hand in respectful greeting.

Confused by this earnest respect for a devastated young businessman of questionable heritage, Algernon stuck out his hand to shake Mr. Sutton's. "A pleasure to make your acquaintance, Mr. Sutton."

"I'm here on the business of the Coxholt-on-Hugh Railway company," Mr. Sutton continued proudly. "I expect you've heard of it."

Algernon had not, in fact, heard of it. Nor of Coxholt, or any waterway by the name of Hugh. He looked toward Mr. Cullen for rescue, but only received a shrug.

"I'm afraid I haven't," Algernon said, and laughed apologetically, giving Mr. Sutton's hand another shake before releasing it. "How may I be of assistance to you, Mr. Sutton?"

"Well, you see, the matter is," said Mr. Sutton, opening the satchel at his side and bringing out a bundle of papers. "Here, may I?" he asked, and spread them upon Algernon's desk. "Are you, Mr. Clarke, the son of Mr. Edward Clarke, who was in his turn the son of Mrs. Eloise Clarke?"

"I am indeed," Algernon said, increasingly intrigued. He leaned forward to look at the papers, but they seemed to be mostly legal jargon and he couldn't make any sense of them.

"That is Eloise Clarke, born Eloise Cropper, who was the daughter of Mrs. Tabitha Cropper?"

Algernon bit back a 'who?' only because he sensed that it might be to his advantage to go along with Mr. Sutton's detailed knowledge of his ancestry. "I regret that I never knew my grandmother, and I am not acquainted with her maiden name nor her mother's name, but I can confirm that her married name was Mrs. Eloise Clarke."

"Then I suppose you aren't familiar with your great-grandmother's maiden name," Mr. Sutton said.

"No, dreadfully sorry. I haven't the foggiest."

"But it does seem that everything else is in order?"

"My other relations?" Algernon asked. "Yes, certainly. May I ask, Mr. Sutton, what all this is about?"

"Well, you see, the records that we have found suggest that Mrs. Tabitha Cropper was born Miss Tabitha Allesbury, daughter of George Allesbury, Earl of Wealdhant Manor."

Algernon wasn't clear on what all this meant, but the mention of an Earldom in his ancestry had him rapt. "Wealdhant Manor?"

"Charming little place in Lincolnshire," Mr. Sutton said, waving his hand dismissively. "Of which, if you will affirm that you are indeed Mr. Algernon Clarke, son of Mr. Edward Clarke and descended from Mrs. Tabitha Cropper, you are the heir."

Algernon opened and shut his mouth, and swallowed. "Sorry, could you say that again?"

"It is our belief," Mr. Sutton said, with great dignity and authority, "that you are the legitimate heir to Wealdhant Manor and the accompanying estates."

A thrill of excitement prickled over Algernon's skin and he gaped at Mr. Sutton for a moment before turning his gape upon Mr. Cullen, who shrugged.

"How do I…" Algernon cleared his throat, trying to wrap his mind around what Mr. Sutton was saying. "If I were to…"

"If you'll just sign here," Mr. Sutton said, with an easy smile. He pushed one of the papers in front of Algernon. "You'll see that this details your ancestry, and all you need to do is affirm that you are indeed Mr. Algernon Clarke, son of Mr. Edward Clarke."

Algernon seized upon his quill, dipped it in ink, and hesitated.

"Mr. Sutton," Mr. Cullen said, putting Algernon's hesitation into words. "I don't believe you've told us the reason for your interest in Mr. Clarke's ancestry."

Algernon put down his quill pen and looked expectantly at Mr. Sutton.

"Oh, but of course!" said Mr. Sutton. "How silly of me. It's very simple, you see. The Coxholt-on-Hugh Railway company is building a rail line which crosses the lands of Wealdhant Manor, the whole hereditary Allesbury estate, and we simply wish to purchase the slender strip of land which we need for the rail line. It seems that the estate has lain empty for years, so it became necessary to track down the legitimate owner, and here you are!"

Mr. Sutton cast a meaningful look around Algernon's meagre accommodations—a cold garret room with not even a fire in the grate in January. "Quite advantageous for all parties, don't you think? An estate for you, a railway line for us, and progress and transportation for the people of Lincolnshire!"

"That seems straightforward enough," Algernon agreed, and took up his pen again. Glancing toward Mr. Cullen, he found that his friend and valet seemed likewise wary but had no certain objections. "Is there, ahem, any money with the estate?"

"Indeed, there is a trust with the estate that has been untouched for nearly a century! Let me, here we are. This is the information on the bank which holds the trust for the Allesbury estate. As soon as we have your paperwork finalised to establish your identity, you can claim your estate and the respective funds. We already have our Act of Parliament—as is customary in these matters—to authorise the railway's construction, you see. You'll sell us the little strip of land we need—hardly anything, railways aren't very wide, after all! Ha!"

Algernon produced an amiable smile at the joke, still hesitating his pen above the paper.

Mr. Sutton went silent, making it clearer that he was waiting.

An estate! Not the Earldom, most likely. Algernon suspected that the title would have been declared extinct if the old Earl had no sons. He wondered, briefly, what had happened which had caused the estate to fall abandoned and why his supposed great-grandmother Tabitha hadn't made a claim upon it.

Quite advantageous for all parties, he thought. This could hardly get him in any more trouble than his current situation: there weren't many fates worse than a debtor's prison, and at the very least this business would delay that fate.

Algernon scrawled his name upon the page and handed it to Mr. Sutton.

"Such a pleasure doing business with you, my dear boy!" Mr. Sutton exclaimed, gathering his papers and leaving Algernon with a stack of pages on the subject of his new estate and the proposed railway line. "We'll take care of this bit of the paperwork. As soon as this is registered, you can draw upon the trust—and then it's off to Wealdhant for you, I imagine! As you see here, this diagram shows the proposed route of the railway line. All of this is your property, from here to here, including these tenants and farms. I'll leave it to you to sort out the matter of their unpaid rents these past decades! Ha! But the thrust of the matter is, well. You see, the railway will cut through some of these farms, and that will need a landlord to sort it out with the farmers resident upon the land… you understand, I'm sure."

Algernon frowned as he looked over the map, but it seemed to him that there was plenty of land available adjacent to the manor, and surely with some money from the estate the farms could be relocated out of the railway's path.

"Some of these people can be very … well, old-fashioned, I'm sure you can imagine! But it is your land, you see, and progress helps everyone! The prosperity that a railway would bring to this area of Lincolnshire, it would be all for the best."

"Certainly," Algernon agreed, nodding as he continued studying the map of Wealdhant Manor and the nearby village of Wilston, most of which was indicated as property of the Allesbury estate. "What the railways have done for England's economy in the past fifteen years is remarkable, and I am myself a devout believer that technology improves life for all of us."

"We are of one mind, then, Mr. Clarke!" Mr. Sutton shook his hand firmly. "It has been such a pleasure to meet you, sir. I shall be in touch very soon."

Feeling nearly dizzy with hope and amazement at this sudden change of his circumstances, Algernon shook his hand enthusiastically in return. "The pleasure is all mine, Mr. Sutton."

Mr. Cullen showed their visitor the three steps to the door, and shut it behind him.

"Well!" Algernon exclaimed. "Wealdhant Manor, Cullen! And me a landed gentleman! What do you suppose?"

Mr. Cullen raised his brows eloquently.

Algernon grimaced. "I am perfectly aware that... well, it's all a bit sudden and suspicious, isn't it? But it's this or the debtor's prison, unless you see any alternatives. And what if I am indeed the heir of Wealdhant? I think it's all very grand, Cullen. This venture will be the making of me, I assure you."

It was very good of Mr. Cullen, Algernon thought, that he did not comment on the fact that Algernon had said the same thing about their last three ventures. He did, however, imply it with the set of his frown.

"Wealdhant it is, then, sir," Mr. Cullen said, and sighed.

* * *

The Two Lords of Wealdhant Manor

will be released by Honeywine Publishing in December 2015.

www.HoneywinePublishing.com

CPSIA information can be obtained at www.ICGtesting.com
Printed in the USA
LVOW10s1855041115

461096LV00009B/825/P